MANUSCRIPTS AND DEADLY MOTIVES

DUNE HOUSE COZY MYSTERY SERIES

CINDY BELL

CONTENTS

Chapter 1   1
Chapter 2   15
Chapter 3   23
Chapter 4   35
Chapter 5   47
Chapter 6   61
Chapter 7   77
Chapter 8   89
Chapter 9   103
Chapter 10   117
Chapter 11   125
Chapter 12   139
Chapter 13   153
Chapter 14   167
Chapter 15   177
Chapter 16   187
Chapter 17   203

Also by Cindy Bell   211
About the Author   217

ISBN: 9781797681924

CHAPTER 1

*T*he cloth glided with ease across the smooth wood. Suzie Allen breathed in the lemon scent and felt her muscles relax. Never would she have believed that she would take so much pleasure in cleaning. As she moved through the room, which had been decorated with a Parisian theme, she admired every piece of furniture and every ornament. The guests who checked out that morning left glowing reviews not only of the room itself, but of the bed and breakfast. It filled her with warmth to know that she and her best friend Mary Brent, had created an environment that was both recreational and restorative. To some degree she believed that Dune House provided people an escape from their day-to-day routine. In essence, it was a place for them to rest and rejuvenate. As she prepared the room for the next guest, she thought about what it might be like to come to Dune House, from their point of view.

Located on a small strip of beach, it was flanked on one side by woods, and on the other by the idyllic town of Garber. The house had once been her uncle's, a man she barely knew, but he'd left it to her when he passed away. Once she and Mary got their hands on it, they transformed it back into its former glory as a bed and breakfast. Most of the rooms overlooked the beach. With three stories, there were plenty of rooms for people to choose from, and Suzie had taken the time to decorate each one with a different theme. It was finally a chance for her to properly express her interests in interior decorating and she had loved every moment.

"How's it going in here?" Mary stuck her head through the door with a warm smile.

"I'd probably be done faster, if I wasn't daydreaming so much." Suzie laughed as she turned to face her friend. "Something about this cleaner always gets my mind wandering off."

"Maybe you should open a window." Mary grinned as she walked over to one of the large windows on the other side of the room. She eased it open and was immediately greeted by a warm breeze, laced with the scent of salt.

"Thanks, that might help." Suzie tossed her a cleaning cloth. "Do you want to polish the windowsill while you're over there?"

"Can do." Mary snatched it out of mid-air. In moments like these, she didn't feel like she was in her fifties. Spending time with Suzie always made her feel so much younger, and Dune House itself brought out that youthful feeling as well. It wasn't long ago that she felt as if her life was coming to an end. Her marriage was over, her children Catherine, and Benjamin were off to college and starting their own lives. When Suzie invited her to Garber and then to help with Dune House it had been a life-saver, and she had never looked back. "I tried checking on Amelia this morning, but she didn't answer."

"I worry about her." Suzie shook her head as she pulled the sheets off the bed. "I know she requested privacy, but I'm not even sure that she's eating."

"She had that pizza delivered two nights ago, but I don't think there's been anything since." Mary cringed. "I hate to think of the state of that room."

"Yes, it will probably need a thorough cleaning when she leaves." Suzie frowned as she shook a pillow out of its pillowcase. "I can understand her passion, her dedication to writing her manuscript, but she's been here for almost two weeks and hasn't joined us for a single meal. In fact, I've only seen her leave her room a handful of times, and I don't think she's visited town at all."

"It is a bit strange, isn't it?" Mary finished the windowsill, then moved on to the second window in the room. "I know she requested privacy, but sometimes I think she needs a little friendship."

"But we can't force it on her." Suzie shrugged and tossed the linens into a nearby laundry basket. "I guess it is best just to let her have what she needs. If that's how she can finish her manuscript, then I guess it's for the best. That's why she came here after all."

"True. Maybe I'll leave her a little care package of goodies outside her room later. I'll slip her a note to say that it's there." Mary glanced over at Suzie. "Do you think that would be all right?"

"I think it would be fantastic. You're so thoughtful, Mary." Suzie smiled at her friend. As they left the room and headed down the hall, Suzie was full of anticipation. The next morning, she would be standing on the dock waiting for Paul to arrive back from one of his trips on the water. As a fisherman, he was often gone for several days at a time. She couldn't wait to see him and find out how his journey went. Mostly, she couldn't wait to get her arms around him.

Lost in thought, she paused at the laundry room while Mary continued down the stairs. She noticed that her friend didn't have as much difficulty as usual on the steps. When she'd first come to Dune House her knees had been quite a big problem, especially going up and down the stairs. But she'd been working on building muscle and seemed to be in less pain. Suzie hoped the trend would continue. She tossed the linens into the washer, got it started, then headed downstairs to check on the living room.

Other than Amelia, they only had two other guests currently checked in. It was mid-week, and the rush usually occurred on the weekend. Since it wasn't quite warm enough for swimming most people spent their time exploring the town, walking along the beach, fishing and hiking through the woods. Their two current guests, Michael and Lavinia had struck up a quick friendship and were out and about together. Suzie sensed a possible romance between them, but they seemed to be quite hesitant to pursue anything more than friendship.

As Suzie fluffed up the couch cushions, there

was a light knock on the door. She straightened up and was about to walk to the door when the knock came again, this time pounding. Something in the force of the knock triggered a sense of anxiety in Suzie. It was unusual for anyone to knock so loudly in the relaxed town, and certainly no guest had ever been so aggressive, but then any guest would know that the door was unlocked. It was only locked at night.

Pilot, their yellow lab, bounded in from another room and began to bark. Suzie winced as she knew how loud his barks could get. Mary ventured out of the kitchen as Suzie reached the main hallway.

"Who do you think that is?" She frowned as another round of even more forceful knocks assaulted her ears. She grabbed Pilot's collar and gave him a few pets. He whined anxiously but stopped barking.

"No one happy." Suzie braced herself as she approached the door. Whoever was on the other side seemed quite angry, and she wasn't sure that she wanted to let the person in.

Suzie peeked through the long, thin glass window on the side of the door and saw a man who appeared to be in his thirties. She didn't recognize him, which meant he probably wasn't a local. Still wary, she eased the door open enough to meet the man's eyes.

"Can I help you?"

"I want to see Amelia Price right now!" He put his hand on the door and pushed.

"Sir, you're going to have to calm down." Suzie wedged her shoe under the door to prevent him from pushing it open any farther. Her heart pounded as she looked into his furious gaze. Whatever he wanted with Amelia, it wasn't pleasant.

"Don't you dare tell me to calm down!" His cheeks reddened as his voice raised. "I know Amelia is here, and I want to speak with her right this second. Amelia!" He took a step back on the porch and shouted up at the windows. "Amelia, get down here and face me!"

Suzie's heart skipped a beat. She had no idea what this man wanted with Amelia, but his behavior made her suspect he could be violent. She glanced over at Mary, whose brows were knitted with concern.

"Do you want me to call Jason?" Mary whispered the question, so as not to further agitate the man.

"Not just yet. Let's see if we can get him to calm down." Suzie swallowed hard. It was nice that her young cousin wore a badge, but she didn't like to call him for every little problem. "Sir, I'm afraid we can't allow you to come in, but if you would like to leave a message for Amelia, I would be happy to relay it to her. All of this shouting isn't going to get you anywhere."

"No, it won't, because you won't open the door!" He pushed against the door again, as sweat beads formed on his forehead.

"If you push through this door, I can assure you that you will be arrested. Is that what you want?" Suzie's tone became sharp and determined. During her time as an investigative journalist she had her fair share of dangerous moments, and she wasn't easily intimidated. "Think it through, pal, because once the cuffs are on, it's awfully hard to get them off."

"All right, all right!" He took a step back and held his hands up in the air. "I'm sorry. You're right." He took a deep breath. "I was a little out of control, but I'm calm now, okay?"

"Okay." Suzie nodded slowly and kept her gaze fixated on him. "Would you like to leave her a message?"

"Yes, fine." He frowned and shoved his hands into his pockets. As he searched through them,

Suzie realized he was only getting aggravated again.

"Mary, can you bring the notepad and a pen off the front desk, please?" Suzie kept her voice pleasant in an attempt to keep the man's anger from spiking again. She also made sure the door remained partially closed. She knew if he saw an opening, he might decide to bolt through the door no matter what she threatened him with.

"Sure." Mary hurried over to the front desk, grabbed the items, then rushed back to the door. She was less accustomed to danger, and she hated anger. She'd been in an unhappy marriage for far too long, and now that she was free of it, she detested shouting and arguing. But she wasn't going to leave Suzie at the door alone for long. She would do whatever it took to make sure that her friend was safe. The cell phone in her pocket was on her mind. She was tempted to call Jason, despite what Suzie said. "Here you go." Mary thrust out the notepad and pen.

Suzie took them and offered them to the man who paced back and forth on the wide wraparound porch.

"Just jot down a note for her and we'll make sure that she gets it. All right?" She forced a smile to her lips. What she really wanted to say was, get off my porch! But she knew that would only make the situation worse. Whatever issue he had with Amelia, the sooner she got him to leave, the better the chance she would have to protect the woman from this angry person. He snatched the notepad and pen, then began to scrawl words across the paper. She could tell from the sharp movements of his hand that he was putting all of his anger into his words. When he was done, he held the notepad out to her. For the first time a hint of guilt surfaced in his eyes.

"Look, I know that none of this is your fault. But you should know you're harboring a traitor in this place. I'm going to make sure that she pays for what she's done. Understand?"

"I know nothing about what business you have with Amelia, sir, but I will pass this note on to her. However, I must warn you, if you come banging on this door again and acting out of control, I will not hesitate to call the police." Suzie held his gaze. "I take the safety of my guests very seriously. So, your best bet is to wait for Amelia to contact you if you wish to speak with her."

"Oh no, I don't need to speak with that coward." He looked up at the windows above him again and sneered. "I wanted to warn her, that's all. Don't worry, I won't be back." He turned and stalked off to the large parking area off to the side of the house. Suzie watched until he was in his car, then pulled out her cell phone and snapped a few pictures of his vehicle, and his license plate. Once he was out of the parking lot, she turned to face Mary.

"Well, that was quite something, wasn't it?"

"It was scary is what it was, Suzie. Why didn't you call Jason?"

"These things tend to escalate when police get involved. Besides, we handled it just fine, didn't we?" Suzie looked down at the pad in her hands.

"You handled it well, Suzie, I almost had a heart attack." Mary frowned.

"We both handled it well." Suzie smiled, then she returned her attention to the notepad. "Should we read it?"

"I'm not sure, Amelia does like her privacy." Mary eyed the handwriting. "But if it's going to upset her, we probably should, so we can prepare for her reaction."

"It's not as if it's in an envelope or even folded up." Suzie skimmed her gaze over the words. It was a short message, but it was fierce. "He's threatening legal action against her if she doesn't stop writing her book. He's included his lawyer's name and phone number." She looked back at Mary. "Just what do you think Amelia has herself involved in?"

"I don't know, but we should find out. If it's going to draw angry people to our door, we need to know about it." Mary looked up the stairs. "Do you think it's possible that she didn't hear any of that?"

"She usually has headphones on while she's working, so yes I think it's very possible. We'd better let her know what is going on so she can decide what she wants to do next." Suzie started up the stairs, with Mary a few steps behind her.

As Suzie approached Amelia's door, her stomach churned. This was obviously not good news, and she had no idea how the woman would take it. But she couldn't shake the feeling that Amelia might be in some actual danger. The man on the porch had been irate, and if he could be that angry with strangers, how would he act towards Amelia if he were to run into her face to face?

Suzie looked over at Mary, then raised her hand to knock on the door. After three swift knocks, she waited for the woman to answer, with the note clutched in her hands. She could have shoved it under the door, but she wanted to be sure that Amelia wasn't too upset by it, and she could tell her the whole story about the man banging on the door.

"Knock again." Mary sighed. "She probably has her headphones on."

"You're right." Suzie nodded and knocked firmly again. A minute or two later, the door finally swung open.

Amelia's plump frame filled the doorway as she looked between Suzie and Mary.

"What part of do not disturb don't you understand?" Amelia crossed her arms as she glared out at the two women.

*a*s Amelia stood in the doorway, Suzie did her best not to let the woman's abrasive attitude disturb her. She'd come to realize that Amelia was simply a blunt person, and she was always going to say what was on her mind, with no thought to being polite.

"I'm sorry for the intrusion, but we just had quite a strange visit from a man who insisted we pass a message on to you." Suzie held out the folded piece of paper. "He was irate, and I was close to calling the police because he refused to calm down."

"Monroe." Amelia rolled her eyes. "It must have been Monroe." She snatched the piece of paper out of Suzie's hand. "I'm sorry that he caused such a fuss. I didn't hear a bit of it, or I would have come down and told him off myself." She scanned the note, then crumpled it up in her fist. "This is ridiculous. People think they can sue for anything these days."

"I know that you like your privacy, Amelia, but if there's anything we can do to help, all you have to do is ask." Mary looked into her eyes. "We both know what it's like to be in tough circumstances."

"That's kind of you, but I don't need any help." Amelia smirked. "This just means that I'm on the right track with my book. Let him have his tantrum, it's not going to get him anywhere."

"We are both a little concerned about how violent he seemed. If you'd like, I could call my cousin Jason. He's a police officer. I can see if he can start some paperwork so that you can get a restraining order. It might be the best way to protect yourself." Suzie reached into her pocket and pulled out her phone. "I'm sure he'll come over as soon as he's free."

"I don't need protection." Amelia rested against the doorframe. "He doesn't scare me."

"Maybe not, but we do have other guests to think about." Mary frowned. "He was quite loud and insistent, I'm afraid that if he came here again, I would instantly call the police."

"He was that mad, huh?" Amelia smiled some, as if it pleased her to know that she'd gotten under his skin. "Try not to worry about it, ladies, he's all bark and no bite. But if you're really concerned, I guess it would be good to get a paper trail started for my countersuit. Go ahead and call him. Just let me know when he gets here, as I'm in the middle of a chapter."

"Okay, we will." Suzie was relieved that she agreed to speak to Jason. As she placed the call, Amelia closed the door and disappeared back into her world. She wasn't the most social person, but Suzie could understand that. She often preferred her own company over the company of others, aside from Mary and a few others. However, Amelia's abrupt nature made it difficult not to think she simply had a strong distaste for people. She placed a call to Jason, who agreed to come over right away. There wasn't usually much crime in Garber, which often left him available. It made her nervous to think of him going after the angry man that stomped around their porch, but she knew that Jason could handle himself.

"I'll make us some tea while we wait for Jason." Mary headed straight for the kitchen. She always found comfort in cooking or cleaning. She loved taking care of people and she was accustomed to disappearing in the routine activity. While her body worked, her mind relaxed, and her thoughts finally cleared. She had just taken the tea kettle off the burner when she heard the front door open.

"Suzie? Mary?"

Jason strode in, his gaze anxious as it swept the hallway and living room area.

"We're here." Mary waved a towel from the kitchen, then made her way towards him. At the same time Suzie stepped in from the side door that led out on to the beach side of the wraparound porch.

"Jason! Thanks so much for coming." Suzie smiled and met his eyes. "Whoever Amelia has herself tangled up with, he makes me very nervous."

"I'm sorry you experienced that, and I want to hear everything in detail." Jason nodded to Mary as she joined them in the front hall. "Are you okay?"

"Yes, he was very irate when he first arrived. He did leave on a calmer note, but the message he had for Amelia was quite hostile." Suzie frowned. "She didn't seem too worried, but we did get her to agree to speak with you."

"Great. I should talk to her now. Is she upstairs?" Jason started towards the steps.

"Wait Jason." Suzie caught his arm. "I have a picture of his car and his license plate, I'll send it to you now." She pulled out her phone.

"Great, perfect. Yes, please send it. Mary, will you show me to Amelia's room, please?" Jason brushed his hands together. "I would like to speak to her as soon as possible."

"Of course, right this way." Mary led him up the stairs to the third floor. As she climbed each step, she tried to disguise the pain that the journey caused her. Jason either didn't notice or was kind enough not to comment. When she reached the landing on the third floor, she gestured to the room that belonged to Amelia. "She's in there, but you'll probably have to knock pretty hard. She usually has headphones on."

"Okay, not a problem." Jason slammed his fist against the door, which resulted in a sharp shriek from inside the room. "Sorry, ma'am." He cleared his throat, shot a glance in Mary's direction, then turned back as the door swung open.

"Ah, you must be my hero." Amelia smiled at him as she stepped out into the hallway and closed the door behind her. Mary barely caught a glimpse of the typewriter on her desk.

"I certainly will do my best to be." He rested his

hand on the holster of his gun and met her eyes with determination. "But first you have to tell me who this man is and why you think he showed up today."

"Monroe Pecalli. He showed up because he's trying to stop me from telling the truth. My newest book has all kinds of details about my co-workers and the company I used to work for. Details that none of them want released. He's no real threat. He has a lawyer." Amelia rolled her eyes. "Apparently, he doesn't know anything about how the law actually works, or he wouldn't be wasting his money. He can't stop me from writing about my own true experiences."

"I'm not aware of the legal details of his case, but I can tell you that it is against the law for him to harass you. I can start the documentation for you to get a restraining order if he approaches you again." Jason pulled up a form on his phone and began to take her information. As he filled out each section of the form, Amelia seemed to be reluctant to give out the details, however with a little coaxing she did provide what he asked.

"Also, there's a woman, Jessica Cate, she is likely working with him on this. They have both threatened me before." Amelia shook her head. "Nothing better to do with their time I suppose."

"I'll make a note of her name as well." Jason looked up at her. "Now, is there any reason for me to believe that either of these people would physically harm you?"

"It's possible, I guess. Monroe has keyed my car before, though I wasn't able to prove it. I had to come here to finish my manuscript because I couldn't get any peace in my home. I have no idea how he found out I'm here." Amelia frowned. "I guess I might have to consider leaving."

"We will do our best to ensure your safety and privacy." Suzie met her eyes. "But if you'd like I can recommend some other accommodation in the area."

"I'd rather stay here. It's such a peaceful place and I'm making real progress on my manuscript." Amelia looked over at Jason. "You'll keep me safe, right?"

"I'll do my best, ma'am." He nodded, then handed her a business card. "Don't be afraid to call me directly if you need anything at all."

"Thanks." Amelia tucked the card into her pocket. "Now, if you don't mind, I'd like to get back to work." A second later, the door closed on all of them.

Suzie walked Jason out to his car, while Mary

headed into the kitchen to clean up after the tea she'd made.

"What do you think, Jason?" Suzie glanced over at him and noticed that his expression was tight.

"I don't like that he was here, and that Amelia is still staying here, but there's nothing I can do about it right now. I'll try to figure out where Monroe might be staying and look into Jessica Cate, but unless he comes back, I can't arrest him. If he does come back, you call me the moment you see him, got it?" Jason met Suzie's eyes. "The moment."

"Yes, I will." Suzie stared after him as he headed to his car and hoped that she wouldn't have to make that call.

CHAPTER 3

*E*arly the next morning Suzie woke up with a smile on her face. The disturbance of the day before was the last thing on her mind as she hurried to dress. Paul would be getting to the dock soon, and she planned to meet him there with breakfast. The sun wasn't up yet, and there wasn't a sound in the house. She was as quiet as she could be as she headed out of the house. She made one quick stop to pick up donuts and coffee, then continued down towards the docks. They had recently put in extra rocks that were used as sea defenses, so it was now easy to walk on the beach from Dune House to the docks. She always enjoyed the walk. It was just long enough for her to settle into her thoughts. When she arrived, she saw that Paul's boat was already in its slip. Excited to see him, she hurried along the wooden planks until she reached his boat.

"Paul?" Suzie didn't want to startle him by just climbing onto the boat.

"I'm here, beautiful!" His voice floated up to her from the interior of the boat. She smiled at the sound of it. He seemed cheerful, which was unusual after a long trip, though he was always happy to see her. He was the first friend she'd made when she moved to Garber and was glad that he was part of her life.

"I brought breakfast." Suzie climbed onto the boat at the same time that he mounted the steps to the deck.

"You're an angel, I'm starving." Paul wrapped his arms around her, then gave her a light kiss. "I've missed you."

"Ha, you probably spent all of your time thinking about fish."

"I might have, but I named one after you." Paul smiled as he quirked an eyebrow.

"I'm not sure if that's a compliment." Suzie laughed as she held out his coffee to him. "Thirsty?"

"Very." Paul kissed her once more, then took the coffee. "It's so good to see you, I want to hear everything that's happened while I've been gone." He led her down into the cabin where they settled at a small table with their breakfast.

Suzie immediately thought of the event the day before. She hesitated to tell him, as she knew that Monroe's behavior would upset him, and he often worried about her and Mary being in the bed and breakfast alone. He'd been better about it since Pilot moved in. Still, she knew he would find out eventually, so she filled him in on what happened.

"You shouldn't have opened the door. You should have just called the police right away." Paul frowned as he studied her. "What if he had a weapon? Or decided to push you out of the way?"

"None of that happened, Paul, we were both fine. The important thing is that Jason is on the lookout for him now, and he will keep me up to date." Suzie took a bite of her donut. "It really wasn't as bad as it sounds."

"It sounds like he would have done anything to get to Amelia if you hadn't talked him out of it."

"He calmed down eventually."

"And what about this book she's writing? Why would anyone want to write something that will get them that kind of attention?" Paul narrowed his eyes. "You should have encouraged her to go to another place to stay."

"There have been many great books written about controversial topics and revealing secrets. If no one wrote about things that would put them in danger, we wouldn't even have the country we're living in now, would we?" Suzie met his eyes with a soft smile. "Paul, don't worry so much. I can handle more than you think."

"I know you can." Paul took her hand and gave it a light squeeze. "I'm sorry. I'm being overprotective as usual. It's hard for me sometimes, being out on the water, and not knowing if you're safe."

"I'm always safe." Suzie squeezed his hand in return. "I'm always waiting here for you to come home. Never forget that."

"I'll try not to." Paul brought her hand to his lips for a light kiss, which left powdered sugar all over the back of it. "Oops." He blushed and wiped it off with a napkin.

Suzie laughed and gazed into his eyes. She adored everything about him, and even though they had their arguments, when it came down to it, she knew she could always count on him.

After breakfast Paul had some things to finish up on

his boat, and Suzie wanted to be back at Dune House in time to help Mary with breakfast. As she walked back towards the house, which sprawled across the top of a small hill, the sight of it took her breath away as usual. It still surprised her that she lived in such a beautiful place. As she drew closer, she noticed something unusual. Someone was on the wraparound porch. It was quite early for a guest to be outside, and it appeared to her that the woman she saw was acting suspicious. She moved from window to window on the ground floor and looked to be peering inside. Suzie's heart began to race as she realized this woman was not one of the guests at Dune House. She was a stranger, and she might be planning to break in. Suzie pulled out her phone and snapped a picture of the woman, but she was too far away to get the fine details of her face.

"Hey!" Suzie waved her hand through the air to get the woman's attention as she ran towards her. "What are you doing?"

The woman spun around for a brief second, then bolted down the steps towards the beach. Suzie shifted direction and began to chase after her. She wondered for a moment if she might be Jessica Cate. As Suzie ran, she pulled out her cell phone and called Jason. She wasn't going to let another opportunity slip by. She panted out the details to him when he answered. As she paused to catch her breath, she realized that she'd lost sight of the woman. Frustrated, she ran back towards the house to check on Mary and the others. She didn't think the woman had gotten inside, but she wanted to be sure. By the time she made it back to the house, Jason's patrol car was already in the parking lot.

"Jason!" Suzie jogged up to him. "I couldn't keep up with her. She's out on the beach somewhere, I'm sorry."

"It's all right, you did your best." Jason frowned. "Did she threaten you?"

"No, when I called out to her, she just ran. But she was looking in all the windows, she was up to something, I'm sure of it."

"I'm going to find out what." Jason barked into his radio as he ran towards the beach. Just then the front door opened, and Mary, with Pilot at her side, stepped out.

"Suzie, what's going on?" Mary tightened her robe around her body as she stepped farther out. "Is everything okay?"

"There was a woman peeking in all of the windows when I came back from meeting Paul."

Suzie joined her friend on the porch. "I think she might have been Jessica Cate."

"Oh my!" Mary frowned. "We should let Amelia know."

"Yes, and maybe she can identify her, as I took a picture." Suzie showed the picture to Mary. "It's not the greatest, but it might be enough for us to figure out who she is."

As they headed up the stairs, Suzie's heart continued to pound. Whether from the run, or the shock of seeing someone spying on Dune House, adrenaline continued to rush through her.

As Suzie reached the second floor, Michael poked his head out of his room.

"Is everything okay? I saw flashing lights downstairs."

"Everything is fine, Michael, sorry for the disturbance. I noticed someone looking in the windows. It was probably just someone curious about Dune House, but it's better to be safe than sorry." Suzie flashed him a warm smile.

"Oh, okay." Michael stared at her a moment longer, then disappeared into his room.

Suzie wasn't sure if he believed her, but she hoped that he would still feel secure. None of the other guests knew about the incident the day before because they weren't at the house to witness it. Both Michael and Lavinia would be checking out the next day. She hoped that they would be able to enjoy their last day, despite the police presence.

On the way to the third story, Suzie glanced back at Mary, who was a few steps behind her.

"Are you doing okay?"

"Yes, I'm fine, don't worry. My knees are still waking up." Mary offered a soft chuckle.

When they made it to the third floor, Suzie walked up to Amelia's door. If she was like any other writer she'd ever known, she guessed she might be up late and sleep late, but since she rarely came out of her room, she didn't really know her pattern. Still, she felt this was important enough to wake her. She knocked softly the first time.

"Amelia? Are you awake?"

The only response was silence.

"You should knock harder, she could already be working." Mary tipped her head towards the door.

"Okay." Suzie frowned, then knocked harder on the door. "Amelia? We really need to speak with you."

There was still no response. Suzie looked over at Mary.

"Maybe we should just wait until later?" She reached out and tried the doorknob. It didn't budge.

"Jason is probably going to want to speak with her." Mary glanced towards the stairs. "I can go down and get the spare key. Maybe she has her headphones on and isn't going to notice the knocking no matter how loud it is."

"I think I need to get a set of those headphones." Suzie rolled her eyes. "I'll go get the key. You stay here and see if you can get her to open her door. I hate to invade her privacy by unlocking it."

"Okay, I'll knock as hard as I can." Mary began to pound on the door, as Suzie headed down the stairs to retrieve the key. On her way down she ran into Lavinia, who was on the landing of the second floor.

"What's going on up there? What's with all the pounding?" She stared at Suzie with wide eyes.

"Oh, we're trying to get Amelia to answer the door. She likes to wear headphones when she works so there is a good chance that she can't hear us. I'm sorry for the disturbance. We had a bit of an incident this morning and we're just trying to get it all figured out." Suzie continued down the stairs, with Lavinia a few steps behind her.

"It's all right, I just wasn't sure what to think. I

tried to say hello to Amelia the other day, and invited her out with Michael and me, but she completely refused and just closed her door. She seems a little rude to me."

They reached the bottom of the steps as Suzie nodded.

"I can see why you would think that, but she's not here on vacation. She's here to finish her manuscript, so I guess she needs to focus only on work in order to do that." Suzie shrugged. "Passion is passion, right?"

"True. But I suppose sometimes it can become obsession." Lavinia headed for the porch, where Michael stood looking out at the beach. Several police officers dotted the sand. Suzie realized that Jason must have organized an entire search party. As she retrieved the key from behind the desk, Jason's partner, Kirk poked his head inside the house.

"Everything okay in here?"

"Yes, I'm trying to get in touch with Amelia so that she can tell us whether that woman was Jessica Cate. Have you found her?" Suzie tucked the key into her pocket.

"Not just yet. But we're still looking." Kirk headed back out the door.

As Suzie climbed the stairs, she could hear Mary still knocking. The force of it caused a vibration through the wall. Was it really possible that Amelia didn't hear that at all? Maybe the woman did hear, and just didn't want to open the door. If that was the case, then she might be faced with a fight when she unlocked it. Suzie walked up beside Mary and frowned as she pulled the key back out of her pocket. She rarely opened a door when a guest was inside, but in emergency situations, she had to do what she had to do. She just wasn't sure if this would qualify as an emergency.

"Hopefully, she won't be too mad." Suzie slid the key into the lock, turned it, then twisted the knob. As she pushed the door open, she heard a sharp gasp from behind her. When she shifted her attention from the door to the room itself, she gasped as well. Amelia was inside, slumped over her desk. It appeared she had been struck on the back of the head.

A strangled scream erupted from Suzie's throat, and she was distantly aware of Mary speaking into her phone, but all she could do was stare at Amelia. It was clear the woman was dead, and there was no way it could have been an accident.

Seconds later Suzie heard pounding on the

steps. She felt Mary's hand on her arm as she pulled her back away from the door. Dazed, Suzie looked into her friend's eyes.

"Suzie, are you okay?"

"She's dead, Mary." Suzie clasped her hand over her mouth to hide a sob.

Jason reached the top of the stairs first. As he looked at the two women, Suzie could see the worry in his eyes. Then he pushed past them, and into Amelia's room.

Suzie's heart dropped as she wondered if the woman she'd chased down the beach wasn't just a trespasser, but a murderer.

CHAPTER 4

Sirens cut through Suzie's spinning mind. More police cars. The investigation was underway, but she couldn't bring herself to move out of the hallway. It was as if her feet were cemented to the floor.

"I should see to the other guests." Mary clutched at her chest and took a deep breath.

"Yes, good idea." Suzie stared at her, as her heart pounded. "How could this happen?"

"I don't know, Suzie." Mary grabbed her hand and gave it a gentle tug. "Come with me, let Jason do the work he needs to do. It's going to be okay."

Suzie nodded faintly. She was usually the one doing the comforting, but she still felt as if she was in a state of shock. As they made their way down the stairs, several more officers passed them, along with a crime scene investigation team.

Mary stepped off the last stair and looked into the anxious faces of Michael and Lavinia.

"What's going on?" Michael's voice was tight. "Why are the police in here? Did something happen?"

"Is everything okay?" Lavinia looked past Mary, to Suzie, her eyes wide. "You look like you've seen a ghost."

"Unfortunately, there's been a terrible tragedy." Suzie cleared her throat. She couldn't just wallow in her shock, she still had a bed and breakfast to run. "The police are going to need to investigate and will likely be here for most of the day." She walked over to the front desk and pulled open a drawer. "Here are some gift cards for the local diner. Please go and enjoy breakfast on us. I'm very sorry for the inconvenience."

"A terrible tragedy?" Michael followed after her as she approached the desk. "What do you mean?"

"Oh no!" Lavinia gasped and took a few steps back. "It's Amelia, isn't it?"

"We can't discuss what's happened." Mary managed to sound confident. "It's best that we don't discuss it until the police have completed their investigation."

"Oh dear." Lavinia shook her head as she folded her arms across her chest. "What happened to her? Was it an accident?"

"Let's go to breakfast." Michael accepted the gift cards, then walked over to Lavinia. "Let's give them time to sort all of this out."

Suzie offered him a grateful smile that faded as quickly as it arose. How could she smile at a time like this? Once the guests had left the house, Suzie turned to face Mary.

"Amelia was murdered under this roof. That means that someone came in here, and killed her, without any of us knowing." Suzie shuddered as she considered the possibilities. What if the killer hadn't stopped at Amelia? "I should have caught that woman!"

"Just take a breath, Suzie." Mary rubbed her hand. "I know this is a lot to take in. I'm upset about it, too, but there's no way of knowing for sure that the woman you saw is the killer. We don't know what happened, yet. We have to wait until we get a little more information."

"It's a good thing that you can keep me calm, Mary. I feel like I'm going crazy over this. I just keep thinking about how this could have happened. What if I left the door unlocked when I went to meet Paul this morning?" Suzie's heart slammed against her chest as she replayed her hurried movements that morning. Was it possible that she had been in such a rush that she overlooked locking the door behind her?

"You didn't." Mary frowned as she looked at her friend. "You never would."

"When you opened the door this morning, was it locked?" Suzie met Mary's eyes.

"I honestly don't know. I've been thinking about that, too. I just can't remember that exact moment. When I heard you shout outside, I came running out, I can't for the life of me remember if the door was locked. I wish I could tell you for certain that it was, but I would be lying if I did." Mary wrapped her arms around her in a tight hug. "It doesn't matter if the door was locked. What happened to Amelia is what matters."

"You're right." Suzie gritted her teeth and tried to focus on Amelia's death. "It seems too coincidental that someone was spying through the window this morning, and then we find Amelia dead."

"It's possible it's connected, but we also have to

consider who else might have been angered by Amelia. The killer came into this house, only went after Amelia, and murdered her. It seems pretty personal to me."

"She did say that her book would anger a lot of people." Suzie sighed. "I'm betting she didn't expect it to take her life, though."

"If she did, she thought it was still worth it to publish the book. I wonder what she was writing about exactly?" Mary glanced up the stairs as a few officers came down.

"I'm sure we'll know soon enough. Once the manuscript is documented as evidence, we might be able to get a peek at it." Suzie began to pace slowly back and forth but paused when Kirk stepped into the house.

"Ladies." Kirk nodded to them both, his expression grave. "It looks like this has turned into a murder investigation."

"Yes." Suzie's throat felt tight as she spoke.

"We haven't been able to find the woman you saw, Suzie. Can you give me a clear description of her?" Kirk pulled out his phone and opened a notepad on it.

"I took a picture. I can send it to you." Suzie

pulled the picture up on her phone. "It's blurry, but it's the best I can offer."

"Yes, please, send it to me. The tech guys might be able to clean it up a bit. We can run it through facial recognition and see if anything pops up." Kirk's phone buzzed as he received the photograph.

"You should see if you can match the picture to the name Jessica Cate. My instincts tell me that was the woman who I chased down the beach."

"I'll see what I can turn up." Kirk nodded to both of them, then headed back out the door.

"What if they never catch her?" Suzie frowned.

"Suzie, Mary, I need to speak with you." Jason came down the final steps of the stairway.

"Do you want some tea?" Mary started towards the kitchen. "I'm sure you could use some. I could, too, I'll just make a pot real quick."

"No, Mary." Jason caught her arm with a gentle touch. "There's no time for tea. I need to find out everything I can, as quickly as I can. Whoever did this is still on the loose."

"What do you think I should do, Jason? Should I ask the other guests to leave?" Suzie frowned and rubbed her hands over her arms. "I can't imagine that they will want to stay."

"It's up to you, Suzie, but one thing is for sure, I

want you to call a locksmith and have the locks changed. It's possible that a key was lost or stolen and copied. Somehow the murderer got in here. It's better to be safe, and have the locks changed."

Suzie's stomach flipped as she gazed into his concerned eyes. Could she tell him the truth about possibly leaving the door unlocked? Despite their age difference, Suzie considered her young cousin a close friend, and valued his opinion of her. She'd never made such a foolish mistake before. He often lectured her about safety and had pushed her to add a state-of-the-art security system, but she refused to live like that. Would he understand if she had accidently left the door unlocked?

"Suzie, are you listening to me? I haven't been able to figure out how the killer gained access. There didn't seem to be any forced entry, and none of the windows are broken." Jason frowned. "That leads me to think that the killer might have had a key."

Suzie lowered her eyes as heat rushed into her cheeks. Once more she replayed the last few moments before she headed out to meet Paul. Had she locked the door? If only she could remember for sure it would make her admission a lot easier.

"Suzie, what's wrong?" Jason leaned a little

closer to her, his voice determined. "If there's something else, you should tell me."

"It's just that I went to see Paul this morning at the docks. I left very early in the morning, before the sun was up. I was in a bit of a rush, I mean, I think it's possible that I might not have locked the door behind me. We leave it unlocked during the day, once we are awake. But no one else was awake, so I would have locked it." Suzie shook her head. "I really don't think I would have left it unlocked, but I just can't remember if I locked it or not. All of this might be my fault."

"Suzie, it's not your fault." Jason looked into her eyes. "Even if you did leave the door unlocked, it's not your fault. Whoever did this had a plan and was going to take Amelia's life one way or another. The important thing to figure out now is not whether the door was unlocked, but who might have had it out for Amelia and why. Changing the locks is the first step in ensuring your safety, just in case you didn't leave it unlocked, but catching the killer is what will ensure everyone's safety."

"Thank you, Jason, but it still feels like it's my fault." Suzie knew that she and Mary would be the best sources of information for him, since they had the most contact with Amelia before she died. "Of course, there's Monroe. He was enraged when he was here. I could see him killing Amelia."

"Maybe, but until we have a chance to speak with him, we can't rule out anyone else. Including the woman that you saw here today." Jason ran his hand back through his hair.

"I sent Kirk the picture I took of her. Unfortunately, it doesn't show much. That's why we went upstairs, to see if Amelia would be able to identify her." Suzie sighed and closed her eyes for a moment. "I'm sorry, Jason, I should have called you the moment that Monroe showed up, then maybe all of this would have been prevented."

"You did the right thing, by the time Monroe left he was calm. That's not an easy thing to accomplish." Mary patted Suzie's leg.

"Try to keep focused, I need to know if there was anyone else at all, anyone who wasn't from around here, or maybe a local who had a run in with Amelia?" Jason looked between both women.

"Well, of course there are the two other guests staying here, but they've barely spoken to Amelia. She wasn't very friendly. She wanted to be left alone. There is also the couple that checked out yesterday morning." Suzie sighed and shook her head. "There's no one else." Suddenly her eyes widened. "Actually, there was one other woman who was here. She showed up and said she wanted to stay. She asked for a tour, but then left. Rose Finley. She wanted to see every room. Of course, I showed her all of the rooms except for the occupied ones." Suzie shrugged. "She seemed like a nice enough person, but she didn't make a reservation."

"Interesting. Do you have any more information about her?" Jason jotted down a few notes.

"Actually, I do. I had her fill out an information card, and I have Amelia's as well, if you want it."

"Yes, that would be good."

"I'll get it." Mary headed to the front desk.

"Amelia was a writer, correct?" He narrowed his eyes as he looked up from his notepad. "Do you know where she kept her computer? We've searched the room and haven't been able to find it."

"She didn't use a computer. She had an old-fashioned typewriter, and normally it would be on the desk." Suzie recalled the last image of the typewriter. When she saw Amelia's body it hadn't even occurred to her that the typewriter wasn't there. "Did you find it in the room?"

"No, we didn't." Jason made a note, then pursed his lips. "If she was writing on a typewriter then there should have been a hard copy of her current manuscript. We also didn't find that. Or her cell phone." He tapped against his notepad. "It sounds like whoever killed her must have taken those items as well. This looks more and more personal the deeper I get into it."

Mary returned with the paperwork from the front desk.

"This is what we have on Amelia, the four guests, and the woman who took a tour." She handed him the papers.

"Great, thanks. Maybe this will help us identify next-of-kin for Amelia. So far I haven't turned up anyone." Jason looked between both of them. "We should be able to release the room by this evening, but you both need to be very aware of what is happening around here. I haven't ruled out the other guests as suspects, and there is still a slim possibility that this was a random killing. Keep the doors and windows locked at all times." He met Suzie's eyes. "All times."

"Yes, Jason, we will." Suzie swallowed hard. She couldn't help but feel responsible for Amelia's death. Maybe the killer would have gotten in some other way, but an unlocked door likely made it a lot easier.

"I'll call the locksmith now." Mary pulled out her

phone. Only then did Suzie realize that Mary was still dressed in her nightgown and robe. It felt as if hours had gone by, but it was still early. In the span of just about an hour everything had changed.

"I'll be in touch." Jason nodded to her, then responded to some chatter on his radio. "Yes, it's clear down here." He walked over to the front door, opened it, then looked towards the stairs. "They're bringing her out now."

Suzie held her breath as two men carefully carried a gurney down the stairs and out through the front door.

Mary clutched her hand as she hung up her phone.

Suzie realized that both Jason and Mary were right, it didn't matter if she'd left the door unlocked, all that mattered was finding out who did this to Amelia.

CHAPTER 5

A few hours later, the house was still. Eerily still. Pilot lay a few feet away from the door, with his head on his crossed paws. Suzie couldn't stop staring at him. Why hadn't he barked? If he knew someone was in the house that shouldn't be, why hadn't he reacted? He knew not to be aggressive with guests, but it seemed to her that he would have sensed something was off. His intelligence had been proven many times, and he was very protective of Suzie and Mary.

Pilot blinked at Suzie but didn't lift his head. She wondered for a split-second if he might feel as guilty as she did. She sighed as she looked past Pilot to the front porch. The guests would be back soon, and she had to have some answers for them. She

doubted that either were going to be pleased to find
out the truth. Then again if they'd asked the right
people while wandering around town, they probably
already knew what happened, or an extremely exag-
gerated version of what happened. Gossip spread
through Garber like wildfire.

"Here Suzie." Mary pressed something into her
hand.

"What's this?" Suzie opened her hand and
discovered a small chocolate chip cookie.

"Comfort food." Mary popped one into her
mouth. "I think we both need some."

"You're right about that." Suzie took a bite of
the cookie, then looked back at Pilot. "You never
heard Pilot this morning?"

"No, in fact when I ran out to see what was
happening, I had to push him out of my bed." Mary
blushed. "He might have found his way there last
night."

"Mary." Suzie tried to suppress a smile. "I told
you about those bad habits."

"I know, I know." Mary slipped her hand into
her pocket and produced a bag of the small cookies,
which they both began to feast on. "But he gives me
those puppy dog eyes, and he keeps my bed so

warm. Still, maybe if he'd been downstairs, he would have noticed the killer."

"Maybe." Suzie shook her head. "We can't know anything for sure. I think if the killer had made any commotion Pilot would have reacted. Whoever did this had to be a professional, don't you think? Or someone who took their time to plan it out."

"I don't know about that. I would think someone that planned it out would have come up with a better solution than a blow to the head. No one else was staying on the third floor and Amelia's room was on the other side of the house from ours, so it's possible we just didn't hear the struggle." Mary winced. "I don't even want to think about it."

"That's a good point." Suzie stood up and walked over to the front door to pet Pilot. "Did you notice anything this morning, boy? Hmm? Did you hear someone who shouldn't have been here?"

"What exactly happened last night?" Michael pulled the screen door open, then held it open for Lavinia to step through. "I've heard some wild stories in town."

Suzie straightened up and Mary came to stand beside her.

"The truth is, Amelia, our guest on the third floor,

was murdered in her room. That's all we can share with you, but I want you both to know that we take your safety very seriously. The local police have offered to keep a patrol car in the parking lot overnight tonight, just in case, but there is no reason to suspect that the killer will return." Suzie tried to keep her voice level.

"Murdered?" Lavinia clutched at her throat. "How awful!" Her eyes skipped in Michael's direction. "Maybe this has something to do with that phone call we heard."

"Excuse me?" Suzie looked between them. "What phone call?"

"It's nothing." Michael waved his hand. "At least I think it's nothing. We were out on the porch the other night, and I guess Amelia must have had her window open. She was shouting on the phone. Something about a will, and that she had the right to do whatever she wanted. She seemed really upset. Lavinia even went up and knocked on her door to make sure she was okay, but Amelia didn't answer." He shrugged. "I figured whatever the issue was, it was her business, not ours."

"Did she say anyone's name while she was shouting?" Mary took a step forward, her eyes on Michael. "Did you hear her call the person on the phone by name?"

He paused a moment, then shook his head.

"No, I'm sorry. I don't remember hearing her say anyone's name. A few curses, but no names. Lavinia?" Michael met her eyes.

"No, nothing." Lavinia smiled. "I can't believe this happened. Maybe I should head home tonight. I'm not sure I'll feel safe here."

"I can bunk with you if you want. I can sleep on the floor." Michael offered her his hand. "I check out tomorrow. I want to stay the night. We probably have to clear it with the police before we leave the area, anyway. On the way in they said we needed to speak to them. I guess they want to interview us."

"I also want to stay tonight." Lavinia frowned. "I guess that would be all right. If you wouldn't mind too much."

"No, I don't mind." Michael smiled as he wrapped his hand around hers. "I'll make sure you're safe, but I'm sure Suzie and Mary are going to do everything in their power to keep us safe, too."

"Yes, we will." Suzie nodded, then suddenly remembered Jason's instruction to keep the door locked. She walked over to the front door, pushed it closed and locked it. "And Mary and I would like to offer you a refund for two nights of your stay, does that sound okay to you?"

"That's quite generous." Lavinia smiled. "Thank you. I have enjoyed my stay here, I want you both to know that. But honestly, I thought this was a safe area. I'm not sure I could ever stay here again knowing that someone was killed here."

"I understand." Mary nodded. "But if you ever reconsider, our door is always open."

Not anymore, Suzie thought. Now, our door is always locked. At least until the murderer is found. As she watched the pair head off to their rooms, she could recall the day that Amelia checked in. They'd had a brief conversation, during which she'd made it abundantly clear that she didn't want to be interrupted for any reason. It was odd, but Suzie understood that she was focused on getting her manuscript done. Why hadn't she asked more questions?

The musical ringtone on her cell phone pulled her out of her thoughts. She saw that it was Paul and answered right away.

"Suzie, what is going on up there? I've heard some crazy stories, I would head straight there but I have some things I have to finish up on the boat. Are you okay?"

"I am." Suzie felt some relief at the sound of his

voice. She filled him in on what occurred that morning.

"I'm coming up there right now."

"No, don't Paul. Finish what you need to do. We are all okay here, I promise."

"Then I'm coming up as soon as I'm done."

"That's fine but take your time."

After Suzie hung up the phone, she found Mary was on her phone as well. When she hung up, she walked over to her.

"It was Wes, he's going to stop and pick up Paul on his way here in a few hours. He wants to look into Amelia a little and see what he can find out about her."

"Perks of a detective boyfriend." Suzie smiled.

"True." Mary grinned in return.

Suzie and Mary kept busy by making tea and snacks for the investigating officers and technicians.

It was difficult for Suzie to keep her mind off Amelia, but as she worked side by side with Mary things began to feel a little more routine again.

"I'm so glad you're here, Mary."

"I feel the same way about you." Mary gave her a light smile.

By late afternoon the crime scene investigation unit had completed their task, and most of the officers had left for the night. Jason pulled them both aside and spoke in a gentle tone.

"I know this has been hard on both of you. The room is clear now, and I had the boys clean it up the best they could. If you need any more help with it, let me know." Jason started to turn away, then paused and turned back. "Like I said, I'm going to have an officer here overnight, in the parking lot. If there are any issues, anything at all, I don't want either of you to hesitate to contact him, okay?" He looked into each of their eyes in turn.

"Yes." Mary nodded. "I'll make sure he has plenty of coffee."

"That's not necessary, but very sweet of you, Mary." Jason smiled at her, then shifted his attention to Suzie. "I mean it, any little thing that happens, I want you to call, and alert the officer outside, got it?"

"Yes, I will, I promise." Mary smiled. "Thanks for everything, Jason."

"Don't thank me until I catch the killer." He gave her a short wave, then headed out the door. Suzie noticed that he was careful to turn the lock behind him.

When it was time to meet Paul and Wes, Suzie made sure she went through several careful steps.

She checked the locks on each window. She ensured that the house phone was working. Then she double-checked that all of the doors in the house were locked. She grabbed Pilot's leash and attached it to his collar. He wagged his tail eagerly. She met Mary on the porch, where she waited with a thermos of hot coffee and a blueberry muffin.

"Ready to go?" Mary met her eyes.

"Yes, I made sure that everything is locked up tight."

"Great." Mary gave her a brief smile, then the three of them walked over to the patrol car. "Thanks for being here." Mary smiled at the officer as she ducked her head down to meet his eyes. "We really appreciate it."

"No problem, ladies." He smiled at them both. He was a young officer, and though Suzie was sure she knew his name, she couldn't think of it at the moment.

"Here's some coffee and a muffin." Mary thrust the thermos and muffin through the window to the officer. "Thanks so much for your help."

"Thank you." His smile grew wider. "Are you two going out?"

"Just for a walk on the beach." Suzie tipped her head towards the trail that led to the beach.

"Alone?" He narrowed his eyes. "I'm not sure that's a great idea."

"No, we won't be alone." Mary waved her hand as a car pulled into the parking lot.

"Okay." The officer nodded, then popped open the thermos and poured himself a cup of coffee.

Wes emerged from his car at almost the same instant that Paul stepped out of the passenger side.

Suzie was so relieved to see Paul that she had to hold herself back from running straight for him. He strode quickly towards her. Pilot strained on his leash to reach Paul and licked his hand as soon as he got closer.

"Are you okay?" Paul wrapped his arms around her. "I'm sorry I couldn't get here earlier."

"That's all right, I'm glad that you're here now." Suzie rested her head against his chest. Most of the time she was a very independent woman, who resisted public displays of affection, but as the sun set along the horizon, all she wanted was to feel safe in Paul's arms.

Mary snuggled close to Wes as they walked together towards Suzie and Paul.

"I still think that it's risky for you and Suzie to stay at Dune House tonight."

"I think it's one of the safest places we can be, I

truly believe that." Mary met his eyes. "We have an officer stationed outside, see?" She pointed to the patrol car.

"Yes, I see, and that's a good thing. But I'd still feel safer if you were with me." Wes tightened his arm around her shoulders. "I hate the thought of what happened while you were asleep in your bed."

"Me too. I can't believe I slept through it. I keep thinking if I had just woken up."

"I'm glad that you didn't wake up. Then you might have been hurt or worse. I don't know what I would do then."

"You're sweet, Wes." Mary sighed, then nodded to Paul as they met up in the parking lot. Wes bent down to greet Pilot and patted his head. Pilot's tail wagged eagerly.

"Hi Mary." Paul gave her shoulder a light squeeze. "Are you holding up okay?"

"So far, so good." Mary nodded.

"She's been like a rock." Suzie smiled at her. "I'm glad we could all get together. I'd love to try to figure some of this out."

"That's my goal. The faster Jason can get this killer behind bars, the safer I will feel. I did a little digging." Wes glanced over at Mary. "I hope you don't mind."

"No, I don't mind at all." Mary squeezed his hand. "Thanks for doing that. What did you find out?"

Suzie let Pilot off his leash so he could run along the water's edge.

"Well, according to everything I could turn up, Amelia has very few relatives. I found her mother in a nursing home up north, but she is no longer coherent. I believe there is still a living relative called Sophia, but I haven't found out too much about her. I only found her because both Amelia and her cousin Sophia were listed in an obituary for Sophia's mother."

"How sad." Mary frowned. "She was nearly alone in the world."

"Aside from the people that were angry at her." Paul shook his head. "How could one book generate so much hate?"

"According to her, the book told the truth about the company that she used to work for, and her co-workers. But she didn't tell us much more than that. Now, we may never know because the manuscript is missing. Jason thinks that the killer took it," Mary explained.

"That makes sense." Wes nodded as he continued to stroll at an easy pace along the beach.

"It's clear that someone wanted her dead and didn't want that book released."

"It seems that way." Mary kicked some sand with the toe of her sandal. "But what if the killer just took the manuscript to throw off the investigation? Or what if Amelia hid the manuscript somewhere else?"

"She might have been afraid of Monroe coming after her again." Suzie's eyes widened. "Yes, that's possible. She might have put it somewhere to keep it safe."

"And the typewriter?" Paul frowned. "I don't think she would have hidden that."

"No, probably not." Suzie nodded and gazed out over the calm water. "Most likely the manuscript is gone."

"But that doesn't mean there is no record of it." Wes slowed to a stop. "She might have kept copies of part of it, or at least an outline somewhere else. However, it sounds like Monroe and his co-workers already had a good idea of what was in that book. Maybe we should speak to him to find out what had him so angry."

"I'm sure Jason has tracked him down by now, but he hasn't let me know what's happening. I'll check with him in the morning." Suzie picked up a shell and tossed it out into the water. It made a solid splash. "I'm not going to be able to let this go. I need to know what happened to Amelia, not just to honor her life, but to ensure that Dune House can continue to offer safety and security to our guests."

"Don't worry, sweetheart." Paul rubbed his hand along her back. "We're going to get all of this cleared up."

"I hope you're right, Paul." Suzie fell into step beside him as the group turned back towards Dune House. Even in the evening light it looked majestic against the sky. Normally, she would say it welcomed her, but now as she gazed into its large windows, she sensed dark secrets swirling around inside. Whatever happened there, the tragedy of it would linger until the crime was solved.

That night as Suzie settled into bed, a shiver of fear passed through her. She knew that it was unlikely that the killer would return, but even a small possibility left her unsettled. Dune House had become her home, and now, she felt a little uneasy within its walls.

CHAPTER 6

*S*uzie woke up early the next morning. She wanted to make sure she was awake before the guests, and even before Mary. She made her way through the house, double-checking the locks. She found that each one was still in place. Then she headed upstairs to the third floor. The entire floor was empty, which gave the silence around her a sense of thickness. She knew that Mary would help her with her task, but she didn't want her to have to go through it. She pulled off the remainder of the police tape from the door and balled it up, then opened the door.

When Suzie stepped inside, she was met by unusual scents. Some bitter, some sharp. Whatever the CSI team had used definitely lingered, along with the fingerprint dust, and the mess they'd made of the room. The bedding had been removed, the mattress stood upright against the wall, and all the drawers were opened, the contents emptied. She could only assume that all of Amelia's personal belongings had been taken as evidence. Despite the relaxing and cheerful nautical theme of the room, a heaviness clung to the walls.

"All right, time to get this place cleaned up." Suzie stepped back out of the room and gathered some cleaning products from the hall closet. When she returned, her breath caught in her throat. She almost expected Amelia to be there with a cross look for having her privacy intruded upon. After a quick shake of her head she set to work on cleaning. A few minutes later she heard footsteps outside the door. Her heart skipped a beat as she looked up.

"Suzie, I would have done this." Mary stood in the doorway, a light frown creased her forehead.

"I know, Mary, but you did so much yesterday." Suzie moved over to the desk, which despite the manner of Amelia's death had escaped any harm. "I just have to polish this and then—"

"Suzie." Mary walked over to her. "Don't you think we should just replace it? I don't think I will ever be able to look at it the same way again."

"You're right." Suzie nodded as she gazed at the desk. It was a favorite find of hers, but it no longer offered the same pleasure as it once had. "Let's see how heavy it is. I can get Jason to help me move it out when he gets a chance." She gave the desk a light tug away from the wall. It was much heavier than she remembered, but then she'd had it delivered. As she tugged the desk again, a piece of paper drifted down from between the wall and the edge of the desk. "What's this?" She reached down and snatched up the paper. It looked like it was a piece torn from a larger piece of paper. A name was jotted across it.

"JuJu Lurue." Suzie held up the paper for Mary to see. "What do you think that means?"

"I don't know, but Amelia must have written it." Mary eyed it for a moment. "Maybe it was someone she was concerned might be coming after her?"

"Maybe. It's a very unusual name. JuJu. Maybe it's a nickname for Julie?" Suzie frowned as she turned the paper over in her hand. On the other side were the initials 'AP' and yesterday's date. She showed it to Mary. "I guess the crime scene team must have missed it since it was wedged between the wall and the desk."

"Maybe that's how it was torn. It got stuck?"

Mary shivered a little as she looked back at the desk. "Do you think the killer might have torn it?"

"I don't know. But I do think we need to find out what this name is about. I'm going to send Jason a text." Suzie snapped a picture of the torn piece of paper, then attached it to a text along with an explanation of how she found it. "I think we're done in here, Mary. Let's go have some coffee. Michael and Lavinia are checking out today, and I want to make sure they have a nice send off."

"Yes, let's." Mary passed her gaze over the room one last time. She hoped that removing the desk would be enough to mute the memory of what happened there.

As the coffee brewed there was a knock on the door. It was light enough that it was meant to not disturb the guests.

"It must be Jason." Suzie started towards the door, and Mary stuck right by her side.

"But it might not be." Mary linked her arm through her friend's. "Strength in numbers, right?"

"Right." Suzie took a deep breath, then peeked out through the side window. "It's him." She smiled and unlocked the door. "Jason, you could have used your key."

"I didn't want to startle you. I got your text, and

I wanted to see the piece of paper for myself and log it into evidence." Jason sniffed the aroma that floated through the air. "Is that coffee I smell?"

"Come in and have a cup." Mary gestured for him to follow her.

As Jason walked past her, Suzie fumbled in her pocket for the slip of paper.

"I'm sorry, Jason, but I wasn't terribly careful with it." She handed it over to him as he settled down at the table.

"Don't worry about that. There's not much chance of getting a print off it, and even if we did manage to get one, it would likely belong to Amelia. I'm curious because I ran that name through our system and it doesn't return as a legal name, for anyone." Jason raised an eyebrow. "I thought maybe the camera had smudged some of the letters, but I can see now that it was an accurate picture."

"It doesn't sound like a real name does it?" Mary laughed a little as she returned with mugs of coffee. "JuJu Lurue? We thought maybe it was short for Julie."

"So did I, and unfortunately that name turns up a few possibilities. I'm going to work on it. I will do some more general searches now I can see the name is accurate." Jason took a long swig of his coffee. "I just thought maybe she mentioned something to you that might stir an idea up about who JuJu Lurue could be."

"No nothing, I'm sorry, Jason." Suzie gazed down into the liquid in her mug.

"I can't think of anything either." Mary shook her head as she looked at him thoughtfully. "I do hope you are getting some sleep."

"Actually, that's not the only name I've had trouble with. The woman you gave a tour to, she doesn't seem to exist." Jason avoided commenting on his lack of sleep. "I've been trying to track her down but haven't had any luck."

"Maybe she wrote down a fake name." Suzie shrugged. "It's strange but people do it sometimes, to avoid getting junk mail or phone calls."

"And the phone number she listed doesn't work." Jason nodded. "You're probably right."

"What about Monroe, have you been able to track him down?" Suzie set her mug down and studied him.

"Yes, he's still in town. He's staying at the motel. When I spoke with him, he seemed pretty upset. He claims to have an alibi, but I haven't verified it yet." Jason stood up from the table. "Thanks for the coffee."

"You're welcome, Jason. Make sure you get some rest." Mary gave his shoulder a light pat.

"I'll try." He winked at her.

"When all of this is over and if you have some spare time, we'd really like to get rid of the desk in Amelia's room." Suzie walked him to the door.

"Sure, I can help you with that." Jason paused at the door and met her eyes. "Keep this locked, got it?"

"Got it." Suzie smiled.

After serving breakfast and checking out their last two guests, Mary began to tidy up.

"The locksmith will be here in about fifteen minutes. I'm sorry, Suzie, I think I forgot to tell you." Mary dried off a plate and tucked it into a cabinet.

"That's okay. I'm glad you made an appointment with him, it had completely slipped my mind." Suzie stepped in to help put away the dishes. "How do you think breakfast went?"

"Fine, I think. Michael and Lavinia seemed content, if not a little happy. Did you notice the looks between them?" Mary grinned. "I heard him say he had something to give her a couple of days ago, and I'm sure she was wearing his necklace yesterday. I didn't notice it today, though. I think maybe they are going to keep seeing each other even though their vacation is over."

"That would be nice." Suzie smiled, as for a moment she gave in to the distraction of romance. It was a relief not to think about Amelia, at least for a few seconds. She sent a text to Paul to let him know she had an appointment with the locksmith. He was going to be busy with errands most of the day, but had asked her to meet up with him for a quick lunch at some point.

Suddenly, Pilot jumped to his feet and ran towards the door. He barked long and low, and stared hard at the door. Suzie followed after him.

"Calm down, Pilot, it's all right, boy." Suzie peered through the side window in the same moment that the man outside knocked sharply. The sound made her jump slightly, but it only took her a second to recognize Charles on the other side. He was the only locksmith in town, and she'd known him for some time.

"Hello Charles." Suzie smiled as she opened the door.

"Hi." Charles eyed Pilot nervously. "Is he all right? He doesn't usually bark at me."

"Yes, he's okay. He's just a little edgy. We all are. Go find Mary, boy." Suzie shooed the dog off towards the kitchen. "Thanks for coming out so quickly."

"Of course." Charles set a small toolbox on the floor along with a plastic bag. "I have the new locks here. It's wise of you to do this. You can never be too careful."

"Will you be able to tell if the lock was picked?" Suzie leaned against the wall as she watched him work.

"Yes, if there is any evidence of a break-in, I should be able to spot it. However, there are some sophisticated lock picking tools that don't leave a scratch behind. Just a second." Charles pulled off the old door handle then began to look over it. He peered at it for several seconds, before he looked up at her. "Nope, it doesn't look like this one was picked. But I'll let you know if I find anything on the others."

"Thank you." Suzie's heart dropped. She had been harboring some hope that he would find evidence of a break-in, so she wouldn't be to blame for leaving the door unlocked. By the time he finished his work all of that hope was gone, as he verified that not a single lock he changed had been damaged in any way.

"Here are your new keys." Charles handed her a set. "If you have any trouble at all just let me know."

"Thanks Charles." Suzie walked with him to the door, and noticed that Pilot stuck right by her side, but this time he wasn't barking.

"Anytime." He tipped his head towards her. "You gals stay safe."

"Thanks." Suzie waved as he headed down the porch, then she looked down at Pilot. "What's wrong, buddy? You've been clinging to me all morning. What do you know that I don't?"

Pilot just gazed back at her, his big, brown eyes unblinking. She had the distinct feeling that he was telling her to figure it out.

"Mary?"

"Yes?" Mary stepped in from the living room.

"I think we should pay Summer a visit."

"Okay. Let me grab my things. Hopefully, she'll tell us something about Amelia."

Dr. Summer Rose was not only Jason's wife, but the town's medical examiner. Suzie knew that by now she might have some information she was willing to share. Maybe it would indicate who Amelia's killer was.

The short drive into town felt like it took longer than usual. Suzie kept her focus on the road, but her thoughts were on Amelia, and also Pilot.

"You know Pilot barked at the locksmith this morning. I still find it hard to believe that someone could have come into the house, someone he didn't know, and he wouldn't be alarmed." Suzie frowned as she pulled into the parking lot of the medical examiner's office. "What do you think?"

"I think maybe he was just sound asleep. If the killer didn't make any noise, he might not have noticed." Mary shook her head. "But you're right, it is a little strange."

When they stepped into the medical examiner's office, Summer had just stepped behind the front desk.

"Suzie, Mary. How are you two holding up?" She looked at both of them with a soft smile. "I know this is a lot to handle."

"We're doing okay." Suzie rested her hands on the counter, then looked into Summer's eyes. "We'd be doing a lot better if we knew a little bit more about what happened to Amelia."

"Ah, I knew this wasn't just a drop-in."

Summer smiled. "I've already finished examining her. But I can't really discuss what I found, you know that."

"Of course." Suzie nodded slowly. She was a bit disappointed, but it was worth a try. "You should come over for dinner soon."

"That would be nice. Thanks." Summer smiled.

As Suzie and Mary turned to leave, Jason pushed the door to the office open. His eyes widened when he saw them.

"Ladies." Jason smiled. "I guess that I shouldn't be surprised that you are here."

"We just wanted to visit Summer." Suzie cleared her throat.

"I actually have some information to discuss with you." Jason turned to Summer. "Is it okay if we use your office?"

"Sure." Summer gestured to the back.

Mary hesitated as they followed Jason and Summer towards the back.

"I would prefer not to discuss the information out in the open." Jason closed the office door as they all piled inside.

"Time of death was between two and five in the morning." Jason picked up an open folder and looked to both Suzie and Mary.

"Two and five?" Suzie tried to catch a glimpse of the report in the folder. "Are you sure about that?"

"Yes, I was able to pinpoint it fairly precisely." Summer nodded. "Why? Do you have a reason to doubt that?"

"Not exactly. I just assumed she had been killed after I left the house. But I didn't leave until a little after five-thirty. I must have slept through the entire thing. How is that possible?" Suzie frowned.

"Don't forget, I slept through it as well." Mary slid her hands into her pockets and shifted her stance. "We all did. She was the only person staying on the third floor."

"There are signs of a struggle, but her death was instant," Summer explained.

"How did someone get into her room." Suzie narrowed her eyes. "It seems impossible. She always kept her door locked."

"Amelia may have let the person in." Mary began to pace slowly. "That would explain why there was no forced entry on the front door either."

"That's a good guess, Mary." Jason nodded. "It's possible that she didn't think she was in any danger. Of course, these are only guesses."

"Thanks for the information." Suzie nodded as Jason's phone beeped with a text.

"I have to get going. I'll catch up with you later, Summer." Jason looked at his phone as he stood up.

"I have other cases to get to." Summer tipped her head towards a gurney with a body bag on it.

"Right, of course." Flustered, Mary headed for the door. Jason and Suzie followed.

"Wait, can I just ask one more question, Jason?" Suzie stopped by the door.

"Sure, what is it?" Jason turned back to face her.

"The murder weapon? Any thoughts on what that might have been?"

"Something large." Jason nodded. "Heavy, and fairly blunt."

"Like an old-fashioned typewriter?" Suzie's breath caught in her chest.

Mary froze by the door. She forced herself to look back over her shoulder. The very thought that Amelia might have been killed by the tool of her trade, made her stomach twist.

"Actually, yes. That could be a possibility. It certainly isn't a common murder weapon but, in the moment, if it was available to the killer, I suppose it's possible. It could potentially match the wound." Summer shook her head. "I can't know for certain without having the typewriter, or at least the exact kind of typewriter. But it's definitely something to consider."

"Thanks for the information, Summer." As Suzie walked through the double doors, with Mary and Jason a few steps ahead of her, her mind churned with thoughts of what might have happened inside that room. Who would Amelia be okay with letting in? Why had she unlocked the front door, and could they be sure that she had?

"I'll catch up with you ladies later." Jason turned in the direction of the police station.

"Thanks Jason." Suzie waved to him.

"That was quite an informative visit." Mary opened the passenger side door of the car, then paused to look across the top of the car at her friend. "Don't you think?"

"In some ways, yes. But in others, I'm more confused than ever. Why would Amelia have let someone in, at that time in the morning? Or did she have an overnight guest we didn't know about?"

"A male companion." Mary nodded slowly. "That's possible. She was in her room alone so often, maybe we just didn't realize she was sneaking a guest in?"

"I don't know." Suzie sighed, then settled behind the steering wheel. Once Mary was in the car, she looked over at her. "I hate to think that I would be so clueless, that I would have no idea what was going on under our roof."

"It's possible, if we were too nosy, people wouldn't want to stay at Dune House."

"Perhaps." Suzie nodded as she turned on the car. "But after Amelia's death, I'm not sure that anyone will want to stay at Dune House, anymore."

"Sure they will, Suzie." Mary gave her knee a swift pat before Suzie drove out of the parking lot. "Dune House is strong, just like us, it can come back from anything."

"Thanks Mary." Suzie flashed her a smile. "That was exactly what I needed to hear." She turned her attention back to the road and felt a little more relaxed. Panicking over what might have been wouldn't solve anything, but trying to find out exactly what happened would.

CHAPTER 7

When Suzie and Mary returned to Dune House, Suzie got out her computer, determined to find a little truth in the middle of all of the confusion. She felt some relief at the thought that she wasn't responsible for the killer getting into Dune House. But that didn't lessen her desire to solve Amelia's murder.

"I think it's time we figured out who JuJu Lurue is." Suzie examined a photo of the paper. "It looks like Amelia wrote this on the day that she died. So, the name must mean something to her. I'm going to see if I can find any connections between the information I know about her and this name." Suzie stretched her fingers. "It might take a little while, but we will find something."

"Let's see, all we really know about Amelia is that she was writing this book. So, perhaps the name has something to do with the book she was planning to publish?" Mary suggested.

"I do see a JuJu Lurue listed as an entertainment reporter. She writes for a few online magazines."

"Why would she write it down with the date and her initials?" Mary frowned. "Maybe it is very important to the book. Maybe Amelia signed her initials and the date on the bottom of each page of the manuscript. I think she would have only had one copy of the manuscript. She used a typewriter and I don't know how she could have copied the manuscript if she never went out."

"That makes sense to me." Suzie began to jot down a few notes on her phone to mention to Jason.

"It was dated the day of the murder, which means she must have jotted it down after midnight. Obviously, she wrote it before the killer came in. What if she was in a bit of a rush to hide her work? She might have gotten flustered." Mary tapped her fingers on the table.

"That's true. I wish that Jason had her phone, then at least we might have an idea as to whether

she called or scheduled a meeting with anyone."
Suzie sighed. "But apparently the killer was too
smart for that. Jason said no phone was found in
her room."

"So, the killer walked in here apparently easily,
without alerting Pilot, or either of us. Then the killer
was allowed into Amelia's room as well. None of
that makes sense unless Amelia knew the person,
and that person knew enough to take her phone, her
typewriter, and her manuscript." Mary pursed her
lips for a moment. "Do you think there's a reason
the killer chose to use the typewriter?"

"I'm not sure. It could have just been what was
available at the time."

"If that was the case then maybe the killer wasn't
planning on killing Amelia. Maybe they got into an
argument, or some kind of fight?" Mary tapped her
chin. "Something caused the visitor to snap, and the
only weapon available was the typewriter."

"It's possible." Suzie nodded, but frowned. "But
it's all just guesses until we find out more."

Mary's phone buzzed, distracting them both
from the dead-end conversation.

"It looks like Wes is headed this way."

"Go and spend some time with him." Suzie gave

her a quick hug. "I'm going to see if I can find out anything more about JuJu Lurue."

"Let me know if you find anything." Mary headed to her room to freshen up a little. As she passed a brush through her auburn hair, she barely noticed the streaks of gray in it. There was a time when she would stare at those streaks in the mirror and think that her life was coming to an end, that the best times were behind her. But she couldn't have been more wrong. Now that she was in her fifties it was as if life had opened up to her for the first time, not as a wife, or as a mother, but as a woman, free to pursue her interests. Just the thought of Wes made her smile.

When Mary stepped out onto the porch, she found his car had just pulled into the parking lot. She watched him approach and noticed the determination in his gait. It was as if he was on a mission. He had on his cowboy boots and a toothpick in his mouth. The familiar sight always brought a smile to her face.

"Mary." He smiled as he mounted the stairs and gazed at her with that same look he always gave her. She wasn't sure how to define it, but it made her feel warm from head to toe.

"Wes, I'm glad you came." She pulled him into a close hug.

"I have some news for you." Wes led her to a bench along the railing of the porch. "Are you ready for it?"

"Is it about Amelia's death?" Mary searched his eyes.

"Yes, it is. I found something interesting."

"Wait, I should get Suzie." Mary pulled away from him and headed inside.

When Mary spotted Suzie in front of the sink, she rolled her eyes at the woman's work ethic. No matter what pressure she was under she always found something to do. Then she realized that Suzie wasn't moving, and the water wasn't on. Instead she just stood there, staring hard through the window that overlooked the rear yard.

"Suzie? Is something wrong? Did you find out something about JuJu?" She walked over to her, her heart in her throat.

"Hmm?" Suzie turned to look at Mary with a far-away look in her eyes. "No, nothing. I haven't looked yet. I thought I'd do some chores to get my mind off it for a minute." She blinked slowly. "Then I just blanked out a bit I suppose."

"You're worrying me. I've never seen you like this." Mary took her hand and rubbed the back of it. "Are you all right?"

"Sure, I'm fine." Suzie smiled and drew her hand back. "I'm sorry. I was just thinking about the few conversations I had with Amelia. You know, I assumed that her standoffish nature was just a personality quirk, but now that I'm learning more about her, I'm beginning to think that she had good reason to have that quirk. In fact, she felt unsafe around so many people, I'm surprised she didn't lock herself away somewhere even more remote."

"What makes me the most uneasy is Jason's assumption that Amelia probably knew the killer. It seems to me that whoever it was had to have a good enough relationship with Amelia, that she was willing to let that person in." Mary shook her head slowly. "I can't imagine a friend betraying me like that."

"You're right and I also can't imagine her letting Monroe in. Not after that scene on the porch, not after we both warned her to be careful. I think the mere fact that she let the killer in proves that it wasn't him after all." Suzie grabbed a towel to wipe her hands, though most of the dishes remained in the sink.

"Maybe not him, no, but what if it was someone that he put up to it? Someone that she thought she could trust?" Mary leaned against the counter for a moment as she considered that thought.

"See, that's the problem I'm having." Suzie crossed her arms. "Amelia didn't seem the type to trust anyone, did she?"

"No." Mary frowned. "But I'm sure there are a lot of things about Amelia we aren't aware of, and that might include a close friend or two. Wes is here, and he says he has some new information for us. I wanted you to hear it, too."

"Thanks Mary." Suzie gazed at her friend. She trusted her more than anyone else in the world. She tried to imagine what it would be like to feel that way about a friend who turned out to be a murderer. The thought made her shiver. To cover it up, she quickly followed Mary out onto the porch. "Hi Wes." Suzie offered him a brief smile.

Mary sat on one side of him on the bench, while Suzie took the other.

"Hi Suzie." Wes nodded to her.

"Now, please tell me you've solved this horrible crime." Mary fixed her eyes on him.

"Not solved, no. But the plot does thicken." Wes pulled out his phone and began to skim the screen.

"It appears that Amelia's cousin, and Amelia were estranged."

"That's not too unusual." Suzie shrugged. "Bad blood between family members isn't necessarily motive for murder."

"No, it's not." He glanced up at her. "But these two had been feuding, so much so that Amelia went through the process to get a restraining order against her cousin."

"Wow, that is more than estranged." Mary frowned as she tried to peek at his phone. "Something really must have turned them against each other. Is that her?" She craned her neck.

"Yes, that's her. Sophia Aubray." He held up the phone so that they could both see the photograph.

The instant Suzie saw her, her heart raced.

"Suzie?" Mary noticed the color fade from her skin. "Are you okay?"

"That's her! That's the woman I saw peering through the window."

"Sophia Aubray, Amelia's cousin? Are you certain?" Wes stood up from the bench and handed her the phone to get a closer look. "The picture you took of her was pretty blurry."

"Yes, the picture was. But I saw her face. I'm

sure it's her. I recognized her right away." Suzie gazed at the picture, and second guessed herself. Was it possible that she was mistaken? After a few more seconds of scrutinizing the image she shook her head. "No, I'm certain. It's the same woman."

"That means that Amelia's cousin is in town. No wonder Jason hasn't been able to track her down." Mary frowned.

"At least she was the day of the murder." Suzie narrowed her eyes. "And why would she come all the way here, without a reason?"

"Oh, she had a reason." Wes sat back down between them. "According to my research the feud between Amelia and Sophia has to do with Sophia's mother's death. She left a large piece of property to Amelia. Amelia has since put it up for sale, and Sophia has initiated lawsuits in attempts to stop her. She wants to buy it, but Amelia wants to get the best price. Some lawsuits are still pending."

"I guess they aren't anymore." Mary rubbed her hands together. "That's quite a bit of motive I'd say. She felt that Amelia took something that didn't belong to her."

"Yes, it could be, and the fact that Suzie saw her here, makes her a strong suspect." Wes tapped his phone. "They were only a few years apart in age, I'd guess they grew up fairly close."

"Maybe Sophia showed up and acted apologetic, maybe she got Amelia to let her in?" Suzie met Mary's eyes. "Even if they were upset with each other, having such a long history together might have been enough reason for Amelia to trust her."

"I think you'd better update Jason about all of this." Mary frowned. "Wherever Sophia is, he'll need to speak with her."

After a little more discussion, Wes and Mary went for a walk along the beach. Pilot trotted along beside them. A few minutes of silence passed, before Wes slipped his hand into hers.

"Mary, I'm a bit worried about this whole situation."

"There's nothing to worry about, Wes, I promise." She gave his hand a light squeeze.

"It's just that you and Suzie are such strong and intelligent people, but sometimes that can get you into trouble." Wes grimaced as he glanced at her.

"Trouble?" Mary grinned. "What trouble could Suzie and I possibly get into?"

"I'm serious, Mary. You should be careful about how much you get involved in the case."

"Wes, Amelia was killed under our roof, while we slept. We are already involved, don't you see?" Mary paused and let her feet sink into the sand. The sensation helped to clear her mind. "We want this solved, so that we can move on, and so that we can feel confident booking new guests."

"I understand that. I just want you to be safe." Wes paused as his cell phone rang. "I'm sorry, I have to get this, it's work." As he put his phone to his ear, Mary saw his entire expression change. He transformed from the relaxed, caring man she was used to spending time with, to a sharp and determined detective. After a few words, he hung up the phone. "I'm going to have to go, I'm sorry. There's a big case, and it can't wait."

"I understand." Mary held his hand a moment longer.

He gave her a soft kiss.

As Wes took off across the beach, she could understand why he was worried about her, but she wouldn't let that stop her from investigating. This was about more than just solving a case, it was about the safety of the guests at Dune House and her future, as well as Suzie's.

As Mary walked back towards the beautiful home she'd come to love, it made her feel angry to think that a killer was allowed inside. The least she could do was make certain that killer was brought to justice.

CHAPTER 8

While Mary and Wes headed off for a stroll on the beach, with Pilot at their side, Suzie dialed Jason's number. She wondered how he would react to finding out who the woman she'd chased down the beach was. Would he believe her or think she might be mistaken?

"Hi Suzie." Jason's voice sounded strained.

"Are you okay? Are you busy?"

"Just frustrated." He sighed. "Do you have something new for me?"

"Yes, I do, actually." She filled him in on what they'd found out about JuJu Lurue, as well as Sophia Aubray.

"Wow, I'll see if there's anything more I can find

out about JuJu Lurue. As for Sophia, I've been trying to get in contact with her. Now I understand why I couldn't reach her at her home or work numbers. She's been here, and she could possibly still be here. It doesn't explain why she isn't answering her cell phone, though. This gives me a new avenue to pursue, thank you, Suzie."

"I hope it helps, Jason. Mary and I were talking, and we think that like you said Amelia must have known her killer. It would make sense that it might have been Sophia."

"In some ways yes, but what I don't understand is why would Sophia stick around and peer in the windows? We now know the time of death was before five in the morning. You saw her near the windows much later than that. So why would she kill Amelia, then hang out?"

"I don't know. Maybe she forgot something that might incriminate her. Maybe she regretted what she did and hoped that Amelia somehow survived? It doesn't make much sense to me, either, but I still think she's a strong suspect, especially since you said Monroe had an alibi."

"I did." Jason hesitated. "But I still haven't been able to verify it. He claimed that he was at a nearby bar, but the bartender said it was so busy in there he couldn't remember all of the faces. And Monroe paid with cash, so there is no receipt to prove that he was there. I've checked the nearby traffic cameras and there are plenty of taxis going to and from the bar, but the cameras don't catch the faces of the passengers. I'm currently waiting for call-backs from the taxi company that operates in the area."

"Hopefully, you'll find out something new."

"At this time, I think we can pretty much rule out the possibility of this being a random killing. Whoever killed Amelia had a personal motive. But until we have someone in custody, I am going to keep a patrolman at Dune House overnight."

"Thanks, Jason." Suzie hung up the phone, with her nerves on edge. Monroe was still a suspect.

Mary stepped through the door.

"Mary, where's Wes?" Suzie looked past her towards the porch.

"He had to go. He got a call about a big case, I think he's going to be quite busy for the next few days."

"I spoke with Jason, now I'm trying to decide what to do next." She settled with Mary at the kitchen table.

"I understand. I feel like we can't learn anything

real about Amelia because we keep coming up to dead ends. She feuded with her cousin, but were they ever close? Did she have any friends? What was her life like at this company she used to work for? It looks like maybe she felt the need to hide out at Dune House. She must have been frightened underneath that tough exterior."

"The truth is there is only one person that we have access to that knew Amelia." Suzie stood up from the table and began to pace back and forth. "Monroe."

"Well, we don't really have access to him exactly." Mary shrugged as she watched her friend travel back and forth. "Jason's already spoken to him, right?"

"Yes, he did." Suzie paused, then looked into Mary's eyes. "Jason is a great investigator, but he didn't know everything we do now, when he spoke to Monroe. I think we should talk to him."

"Suzie." Mary stood up and wiped her palms across her jeans. "I don't think that's wise. Do you remember how angry he was when we first saw him? I really thought he was going to bash the door right in."

"I remember." Suzie nodded and began to pace again. "That's exactly why we need to speak to him.

92

He knows enough about the book, and Amelia, that he was willing to risk getting arrested to get to her. That's the kind of information we need. He might be more willing to talk to us, instead of Jason."

"But what if he's the one who killed her?" Mary gasped and shook her head. "I don't think I could handle being near him, knowing what he did."

"Jason doesn't consider him a strong suspect, I don't think. He said Monroe has an alibi. But he hasn't been able to verify it yet." Suzie frowned. "It's possible that it's fake. I can't guarantee you that he's not the killer. But I think he'll be our best source of information. Trying to get Amelia's angry cousin to talk might prove to be very difficult. At least we've met Monroe before. I think he's the best place to start."

"Okay, okay." Mary cleared her throat. "Let's do it. Let's go now, before I lose my nerve."

"Are you sure, Mary? You can stay here." Suzie gave her hand a gentle squeeze. "We both don't have to go."

"We absolutely do both have to go. I'm not letting you talk to that man alone." Mary linked her arm through Suzie's. "We're in this together, remember? No matter what."

"I remember." Suzie gazed at her a moment and

wondered if she would be putting her friend in danger.

"Should we have Wes tag along?"

"No, I don't think so. He's very busy right now with this new case. If things get hairy with Monroe, we can always call him or Jason, we'll be fine." Suzie forced a smile. "I promise."

"Okay, if you say so." Mary rolled her eyes and laughed a little but headed for the door. The sooner they got to Monroe's motel room the better.

The drive to the motel was quick and familiar. Suzie had been there a few times since she'd moved to Garber. The owner was a friend. She was easily able to get Monroe's room number, and he confirmed that Monroe was still staying there. Once she had the room number though, her nerve faltered some. He had been quite aggressive when he tried to force his way into Dune House. She joined Mary outside the office, on the sidewalk.

"Well?" Mary looked at her with a raised eyebrow. "Is he still here?"

"Yes, he is. There." Suzie pointed to the room at

the end of the row. "And that's his car parked out front."

"So, he's here." Mary rubbed her hands together and took a breath. "Let's do this."

"Mary, wait. We should have a plan. Just in case things don't go as smoothly as we hope. He is a big guy." Suzie reached into her purse and pulled out her cell phone. She slid it into her pocket. "Make sure your phone is easily accessible, and if anything seems off don't hesitate to call Jason."

"I won't." Mary tucked her phone into her front pocket.

The two friends exchanged a brief look of uncertainty, then Suzie nodded.

"Let's see what he has to say." She walked to the end of the row of motel rooms and proceeded to knock on the door. For a moment she wondered if he might not answer, but a second later the door jerked open, and Monroe's thick frame filled the doorway.

"You two?" He raised his eyebrows as he stared at them. "What are you doing here?"

"We wanted to stop by and offer our condolences." Suzie did her best to keep a straight face as she tried to fill her eyes with sympathy.

"You're kidding me, right?" He grinned and shook his head. "You're not that dense."

"We know you were upset with Amelia, but that kind of anger usually comes from caring about someone at some point, and we just wanted to be sure that you were handling it okay." Suzie smiled.

"I'm dancing inside, absolutely dancing. Now she can't spread her lies any longer. Why would I be upset about that?" Monroe shrugged. "No skin off my nose."

"May we come in?" Suzie offered her best smile as she met his eyes. She knew the more comfortable he felt, the more likely he would talk. He hesitated for a moment, then nodded and stepped back from the door.

The motel room was sparse with only a bed and a small desk with a chair. The kitchenette was just a counter with a small coffee pot and a tiny sink. He stood near the door. His eyes flitted back and forth between the two women.

"Who's this?" Mary smiled as she pointed to a small frame on the bedside table.

"No one." He grabbed up the frame, but not before Suzie could catch sight of it. Her heart skipped a beat. She recognized that face.

"Who is that, Monroe?" Suzie took a step towards him, her body tense. "What is her name?"

"It's none of your business." Monroe scowled at her and took a step back. "I think you need to leave. This was a bad idea." He started to pull open the door again. Suzie stood in his way, her shoulders squared.

"I'm not going anywhere until you tell me who that is in the photograph."

"Suzie, what's wrong? Do you know her?" Mary moved closer to her, as her heart slammed against her chest. She could tell by the tension in his body and the gleam in his eyes that Monroe was becoming more and more aggravated.

"Monroe?" Suzie stared at him. Then she reached into her pocket and pulled out her phone. "Either you tell me who she is, or I'm calling the police right this second, because I know the two of you had something to do with Amelia's death."

"You go right ahead and call the police. You can't threaten me. I know my rights. I have an alibi for that night, I was at a bar until four, and stood outside waiting for a taxi until five. You can't pin any of this on me." His voice grew louder with every word he spoke.

"An alibi that won't stand up, not for a second. Just tell me the truth, who is this woman in the photograph and how do you know her?" Suzie gritted her teeth, unwilling to back down. From the corner of her eye she noticed Mary's hand slip into her front pocket. She was tempted to tell her friend not to call Jason, but she didn't want to distract Monroe, who was growing more furious with every second.

"You're crazy! I didn't need to kill that woman. I was going to sue her for every penny she had. I don't care what happened to her, or why she is dead, all that matters is that she is gone, and yes that sure does solve all of my problems. Except for the problem of having the two of you in my motel room." He snarled as he took a step towards Suzie.

"Don't you dare!" Mary dropped her purse and held up a can of pepper spray.

"Mary?" Suzie gasped in surprise.

"Put that away!" Monroe held up his hands. "I wasn't going to do anything. You two are the ones who came in here accusing and threatening me! I'm calling the police right now." He snatched his cell phone out of his pocket, though kept his other hand in the air.

"Mary, it's okay." Suzie shook her head slightly. "We don't need that."

Mary pursed her lips but did as she was instructed.

"Now Monroe, I'm just asking you a simple question. There's no need for you to be so upset by it. Please, just tell me, what is her name? I saw her, she was here, she was using a false name," Suzie explained.

"No, she wasn't." Monroe huffed. "She hasn't been here at all. I came by myself to talk some sense into Amelia."

"So, you didn't know she was here?" Suzie tilted her head to the side as she stared at the picture. "I know that's the same woman who took a tour of Dune House. I guess I'm not the only one she lied to. Is she your girlfriend?"

Monroe stared at her, confusion evident in his expression.

"You're just trying to trick me."

"No, I'm not. It's pretty simple, I just recognize the woman in that photograph, and I want to know who she is. That's all." Suzie shrugged.

"Yes, she's my girlfriend." Monroe slid his phone back into his pocket. "When was she here?"

"A few days before you were. She told me she was interested in renting a room. Never mentioned a word about knowing Amelia. Did she know her?"

"I need to find out what's going on. I need to call Jessica. You two need to leave." Monroe gestured to the door again, and this time Suzie could see the determination in his eyes. If she refused to leave, he would grow more and more irate.

"All right, we're leaving. But keep in mind I'm telling you the truth. Your girlfriend, Jessica was it? She is the one who is keeping you in the dark." Suzie grabbed Mary's arm and guided her out through the door ahead of her.

"Suzie, you pushed that a little too far." Mary frowned as she followed her down the sidewalk. "I thought he was going to attack you."

"I had no idea you were smuggling pepper spray." Suzie winked at her. "Tough lady."

"Wes gave it to me." Mary sighed. "Sorry, I shouldn't have done that."

"No, your instincts were good. I just needed to get him to say her name."

"What difference does that make?" Mary shrugged.

"Jessica. He said her name is Jessica." Suzie opened the door to her car. "As in, Jessica Cate."

"Do you really think so?" Mary gasped.

"Yes, I do, and I know she's Rose, the same woman that visited Dune House for a tour. Now we know, Monroe's alibi won't hold water, Amelia's cousin Sophia was skulking around outside of Dune House, and Jessica Cate pretended to be someone else, just to get close to her."

"It didn't seem as if Monroe had any idea about it either." Mary shook her head. "But that could be him covering up for them both. We'd better let Jason know what we discovered."

"Yes, let's stop by the police station on the way back to Dune House."

CHAPTER 9

The small police station was filled to the brim with activity. In the town of Garber, it was very unusual for so many arrests to be made. But it appeared that something was in the air as a few people were escorted through the small station in handcuffs.

Suzie considered speaking to Kirk about it, but he had two people in handcuffs beside his desk. She didn't recognize either of them. As she and Mary were led to Jason's office, she prepared herself for how he might react to the fact that they'd gone to visit Monroe.

Jason gestured for them to sit, and Suzie rushed to give him the update of what she and Mary had discovered.

"What you're saying is you believe this Jessica Cate, who happens to be Monroe's girlfriend, was the woman who toured Dune House?" Jason took a small bite of an overstuffed sandwich, then made a note on the folder in front of him. "Sorry, I haven't had much time for lunch."

"It's okay, Jason, you need to make sure you are taking care of yourself." Mary frowned as she studied him.

"I am, I am." He took another bite, then looked up at Suzie. "You're certain?"

"Yes, the woman in the picture was the woman I met, and Monroe called her Jessica. You remember when Monroe first came to the house causing trouble and Amelia told us that a woman named Jessica Cate might show up, too? I had no idea that she had already been there." Suzie shook her head. "I can't explain why she was there, or why Amelia's cousin was spying on Dune House after Amelia died. Any thoughts?"

"Not just yet. I was able to verify through cameras that Monroe was at the bar, but not what time he left or what taxi service picked him up. His alibi is good until about one in the morning, which gives him plenty of time to return to Dune House."

He set his sandwich down, with only a few bites taken out of it. "You say Monroe had no idea she was here?"

"He claimed to have no idea." Mary leaned closer. "He could be lying."

"Yes, he could be." Jason met her eyes. "Listen, the two of you shouldn't have gone to see him alone. And did I hear you say you went inside his motel room?"

Mary glanced over at Suzie, who didn't say a word. She looked back at Jason with a strained smile.

"We were perfectly safe, Jason. The important thing is we found out that Jessica Cate should be a suspect."

"Which, I already knew." Jason flipped a page in the folder in front of him. "I was already looking into Jessica Cate because she and Amelia have a history. Amelia mentioned Jessica Cate when I saw her about the incident with Monroe. Jessica was Amelia's former boss. Amelia worked at Jessica Cate Public Relations. Amelia was let go due to issues between her, Jessica and a few of the other staff members, including Monroe. As soon as Amelia was murdered, I began investigating Jessica

Cate, because that is what I'm supposed to do." He grabbed his sandwich for another bite, but before he took it, he looked up at both of them. "Why do you think the station is so busy today?"

"I don't know, I was wondering that myself." Suzie frowned as she detected frustration in his voice. Did Jason think she didn't have faith in his ability to solve the case?

"Because I have rounded up every single person that was at that bar, on the streets, or involved in a petty crime within the time frame of Amelia's death. That's how seriously I am taking this investigation. Your safety was compromised, and I can't rest until I know that it won't be again." Jason set the sandwich down again. "I can't exactly stay focused on the case if I'm worried about the two of you getting hurt. Can I?" He stood up from the desk, walked around it, and leaned against the front of it. "I have a police car outside of Dune House every night, do I need to have someone tailing the two of you as well?"

"Jason, you wouldn't." Suzie narrowed her eyes. She knew he was coming from a kind place, but his words sounded more like a threat to her.

"If I hear you went to speak to Monroe again, I will." Jason folded his arms across his chest, a tell-tale sign that the discussion was over. Suzie had come to know Jason's moods fairly well, and though most of the time he was mild and patient, there were moments when she knew better than to push things.

"Let's go, Mary." Suzie stood up from her chair. "Jason has a lot of work to do."

"First, you need to finish that sandwich." Mary frowned and pointed to his stomach. "You're getting skinny."

"That's not true at all and you know it, Mary." A smile twitched its way up onto his lips.

"Eat." Mary eyed him with a look more intimidating than he could ever summon.

"Yes, ma'am." Jason cleared his throat, then picked up his sandwich.

As Suzie and Mary headed out the door, Suzie heard him take another bite.

"Can you believe this?" She frowned and held the door to the parking lot open for Mary. "How can he threaten to put a tail on us?"

"What did you think he would do?" Mary shrugged. "We did take a huge risk by going inside Monroe's motel room, you know it, and so do I. I was scared."

"So was I," Suzie murmured. "I hate to admit it,

but for a few seconds there I thought I'd really gotten us into something dangerous."

"You didn't get us into anything." Mary slung her arm around her shoulders. "I was right there with you. But you can't blame Jason for wanting to protect us, can you?"

"No, I suppose not." Suzie opened the car door. "But it also isn't going to stop me from finding out more about Jessica Cate."

"Do you think we can really find out more than Jason has?" Mary settled in the passenger side.

"Only one way to know." Suzie headed back to Dune House. The quiet streets of Garber were dotted with small clumps of residents. She guessed they might be discussing the murder, and the police round-ups. Jason certainly was taking things seriously, and she was grateful for that, but the faster the murder was solved, the better, and if she could do anything to help with that, she would.

While Mary took Pilot for a walk on the beach, Suzie settled at her computer and began digging into Jessica Cate's business, Jessica Cate Public Relations. She found out that it was a medium sized business with a head office a few towns over. Suzie looked further into the company hoping to find the secrets that Amelia was going to expose.

"Have you found anything?" Mary joined Suzie at the table, while Pilot trotted over to lick Suzie's hand.

"Hi buddy." Suzie gave him a good scratch behind his ear. "Not much." Suzie explained what she had found.

"So this must be the company that she was writing the book about."

"It must be." Suzie nodded. "Jason mentioned that Amelia was let go due to issues with management. So, maybe she was fired because she was on to something." She shook her head slowly.

"I agree."

"It is a public relations company. I imagine bad publicity wouldn't be good for the company. Even though they do say any publicity is good publicity." Suzie glanced at the time on her computer. "Oh dear, if I'm going to say goodbye to Paul before he leaves for his next trip, I'd better hurry."

"Tell him I say to stay safe, please. I'll keep looking into Jessica and her company while you are gone." Mary switched from her seat to Suzie's. "Maybe, I'll come up with something."

"Great, thanks." Suzie smiled, then headed out the door.

Since the weather was warm, and Suzie did her best thinking while walking, she decided to go down to the dock on foot. With her hands slipped into her pockets she walked along a familiar path towards Paul's boat. As much as she enjoyed seeing him, saying goodbye to him before he went out on a trip was always bittersweet. She was happy for him because he loved his work, but also nervous because storms could come up at a moment's notice. She made her way along a rocky trail that led down the side of the small hill that Dune House perched on.

Prior to her small-town life in Garber, she lived in fairly bustling cities. She had grown very used to the refreshing beach air, and the beautiful views of Garber. In general, it was a peaceful place, and she hoped that soon it would be again. As she neared the road, she spotted a few cars parked along the side. It was likely they were kayakers, or boaters, and had gone out for a day trip on the water. She could see drag marks in the sand on the other side of the road, where boats had been pushed in. It was a popular place to launch as it was on the other side of the dock, away from the larger boats, and an easy slope into the water.

"Suzie." Paul jogged up to her from the office at the end of the dock. "I was hoping to have a chance to see you."

"I'm sorry, I lost track of time." Suzie pulled him into a tight hug. "Are you all set?"

"As set as I can be. I wish I could get out of this, but I can't. I hate leaving you at a time like this." Paul brushed her hair back from her face and looked into her eyes. "I'll stay if you ask me to, I don't care what it takes."

"No." Suzie smiled and cupped his cheeks. "I'll be fine, you know that. Your job is important, and besides that, there's not much to do here. Jason is questioning or has arrested half of Garber and half of a few other towns, I think. He's on top of this. You don't have to worry."

"But I still will." He frowned. "And yes, I know you'll be fine, but the thought of being out on that water and something happening—"

"Nothing's going to happen." Suzie stroked his cheek, then hugged him again. "You just focus on being safe out there. I will be just fine. I have lots of people looking out for me."

"Yes, that's true." Paul kissed the top of her head and held her a moment longer. "I just have a few things left to do on the boat before I head out. Do you want to join me and give me an update?"

"Yes, absolutely." Suzie followed him to his home. She could still remember the first time she'd seen him on the boat. It seemed so strange to her to live a life like that, but now she couldn't picture him any other way. He had the salt of the sea in the taste of his skin, and the sun had etched deep lines along the corners of his eyes. His face was weathered by the wind. He was a truly unique man, not only in his looks, but in his endearing personality.

"I want to hear every detail." Paul checked his instruments over as he listened to Suzie's updates. "Wait, are you serious?" He looked over at her. "You went into Monroe's motel room?"

"Just for a minute." Suzie blushed as she realized maybe she should have left that part out.

"Did Jason talk some sense into you?" Paul raised his thick eyebrows as he walked over to her.

"It was a mistake, it won't happen again." Suzie laughed and wrapped her arms around his waist. "Trust me, I already got an earful from Jason."

"I'm sure you did." Paul frowned as he studied her expression. "There's nothing funny about being alone with a murder suspect."

"I wasn't alone, and did you know that Mary

had pepper spray?" Suzie grinned, unwilling to let his serious tone get under her skin. "We can handle ourselves, you know that."

"Yes, I do." Paul sighed and gave her a light kiss. "So, what is your next step?"

"I think we need to find out for sure if Jessica Cate is still in town. If Jason isn't able to find her, he won't be able to question her. He hasn't been able to find Sophia either. He's going to hit some complete dead ends soon if we don't find either of them." Suzie released him. "Don't let me distract you from your final check."

"Yes, you're right." Paul turned back to his instruments and began to go through them again. "How do you plan to find her?"

"I figure, if we tail Monroe, then he might lead us to her. If he cares about her as much as he seems to, I'm guessing he will not rest until he knows what really happened and why she was here." Suzie leaned back against the wall and watched as he marked off a checklist.

"Following Monroe seems like a dangerous idea." Paul cast her a brief look.

"We won't get caught, and we won't say a word to him. It'll be fine." Suzie smiled. "Trust me, I learned my lesson when I was in that motel room."

"I hope so." Paul held her gaze, then returned to his task. "Just think things through and make sure you're not putting yourself in danger. That's it, that's the extent of my lecture." He turned back to face her. "Now give me a hug and a kiss that will last me two days, hmm?" He slipped his arms around her.

"How about a week?" Suzie grinned and obliged his request. As he walked her out to the dock, she gave him another hug. "Take lots of pictures for me. You know how I love the sunsets you see."

"I will." Paul brushed his lips along her forehead, gave her one more squeeze, then finally released her. "Love you."

"Love you, too." Suzie watched until the boat was out of the harbor. As she headed down the dock, she looked up to see a familiar man walking towards her. She smiled at the sight of him.

It was Bill. He was wearing his usual overalls and a t-shirt. He was in charge of the docks, but never lorded that role over the fishermen.

"Hi Bill, how are you?"

"Good Suzie. I heard what happened at Dune House. How are you holding up?"

"Okay." Suzie nodded. "Bill, have you seen anything suspicious around the docks?"

"No." He looked thoughtful for a minute then shook his head.

"If you do will you give me a call, please?" Suzie smiled.

"Sure, I'll let you know." Bill nodded.

Suzie thanked him then headed back across the street.

As Suzie picked her way through the rocks along the path she thought about Paul's warning. His instincts were always good. Was it too much of a risk to follow Monroe? Sometimes her drive to find out the truth drove her right into dangerous situations. However, she wanted the murder to be solved before the weekend. There would be new guests arriving, and they would hear the chatter throughout the town about what happened there. She wanted to be able to tell them that the crime had been solved, and that they were safe in Garber. Although it appeared that the killer was motivated to only go after Amelia, she couldn't be certain of that.

Lost in thought, Suzie stumbled over a larger rock and grabbed on to a stretched-out branch to steady herself. As she did, she noticed something smeared on some nearby rocks. Was that ink? Curious, she leaned down. It looked like ink. Her heart began to race. This indicated which way the killer had probably fled after the murder. Maybe there was a boat waiting for the killer at the dock? Maybe a car parked at the end of the path, on the road? Knowing the direction that the killer went in could prove to be helpful. Excited at the thought, she headed back to Dune House, eager to share the update with Mary.

CHAPTER 10

Suzie pushed through the front door of Dune House and discovered an excited dog on the other side. She laughed as Pilot jumped up against her legs and nuzzled her stomach. He was well-trained not to jump up on guests, but Suzie didn't mind the behavior much at all. She gave him a few minutes of affection, then looked up as Mary walked in from the kitchen.

"How is Paul? Is he off?"

"Yes, it's just a short jaunt this time, he'll be back by tomorrow night." Suzie stretched her arms above her head to try and get energized. "I have something interesting to share with you."

The two women settled at the table and Suzie

explained what she had seen and shared her theory about how it ended up there.

"That makes sense. Maybe the killer tripped, or stumbled, and tried to stop themselves from falling. Or maybe they wiped their hand on the rock to try to clean it off." Mary tapped her chin as she considered the possibilities. "I wonder if Jason might be able to find anything out there."

"I'm going to call him now and let him know. He'll probably want to take a look around."

While Suzie dialed his number, Mary disappeared back into the kitchen.

Jason picked up on the third ring.

"Hey Suzie, how are you doing?"

"I'm okay, thanks Jason. I found something that I think might help the case." Suzie launched into her description of what she had seen and the location where she had seen it, then shared her theory of what it meant as well.

"This is really good information, thanks Suzie. I'm going to send some crime scene investigators out there to process the scene. We might just get lucky and find some physical evidence related to the killer."

"Great. I hope you are able to find something."

Suzie paused. "Any other updates? Have you been able to find Sophia? Or Jessica?"

"Unfortunately, we still haven't located Jessica or Sophia. We are still following up on a few leads." Jason sighed.

"Jason, you sound exhausted." Suzie frowned.

"I know, I'll rest when the killer is behind bars."

"Speaking of that, I thought maybe the killer might have had a boat stowed at the dock, or a car waiting at the end of that path. Ever since it's been built, I use it all the time to cut through to see Paul."

"Yes, that's a good idea. I'll check with the harbormaster to see if there are any records from that morning, and also whether anyone noticed anything suspicious. In the meantime, stay safe, Suzie."

"I will, Jason, and try to get some rest." Suzie hung up the phone, then stared down at the screen. Yes, they had a few suspects, but Monroe was the only one they could locate. It was proving difficult to investigate the murder, when she couldn't speak to the suspects.

"Here you go, Suzie." Mary set down a cup of tea beside her.

"How did you know?" Suzie looked up at her with a warm smile. "This is just what I needed."

"Oh, I can tell." Mary sat down beside her. "I can also see those wheels turning in your head. What are you thinking?"

"I'm thinking we need to find Sophia. I know she was there that morning. Yes, Jessica came for a tour under a false name, but that was a few days before Amelia died. Sophia was there that morning and acting very suspicious. I want to know why. The fact that neither of them are anywhere to be found is another indication that they both have something to feel guilty about. But is one of them feeling guilty about committing a murder?" Suzie shook her head, then took a small sip of her tea. The heat singed the tip of her tongue. She blew across the surface of the caramel shaded liquid, then looked up at Mary. "The only way we're going to help solve this is if we find one or both of them. I think our best bet is to go after Sophia. We already know that Amelia had a restraining order against her."

"How are we going to find her? Jason hasn't been able to track her down. We haven't been able to find out anything either." Mary glanced up at the ceiling for a moment, then looked back at Suzie. "What about the mother?"

"The mother?" Suzie shrugged. "What do you mean?"

"Sophia's mother was the reason that the two women were fighting. She is the main connection between the two women, other than them being cousins. Maybe if we back track from the mother and follow what we can find from her to each woman, we might come across something of interest." Mary pulled out her phone. "What do you think?"

"I think you're brilliant, Mary, but that doesn't surprise me in the least. Let's see what we can find." Suzie picked up her phone. "I have the name of Sophia's mother, and her father, though he passed away when she was young."

"I'll track the father, we might be able to find some information that way, too."

The two sat in silence for several minutes, only speaking up when they came across something interesting. As Suzie began to connect the dots between Sophia's mother and her financial history, something caught her attention.

"I think I might have found something." Suzie held out her phone to Mary. "A property, only a few towns over. Sophia's mother owned it for many years. Sophia inherited it."

"Is it the property that Amelia and Sophia were fighting over?" Mary peered at the address.

"I don't think so. That was listed with a different address, out of state, and was worth quite a bit more. This one is being transferred into Sophia's name. It's still in the process of being changed over, it's possible that Jason didn't turn it up in his search. It's about an hour away from here. If Sophia was going to hide out anywhere, my guess is that it would be here."

"Should we let Jason know?" Mary frowned. "He might be able to have the place searched."

"That's what I'm concerned about. If she sees the police coming, she might run, and we might never have the chance to speak with her. But if she sees a regular car pull up, someone she probably doesn't recognize walking around, that hopefully won't be enough to spook her. Plus, it may be a dead end, and then more of Jason's time and resources will have been wasted. I think one of us should take a drive out there, just to see what's going on. We don't have to speak to her this time, but if we find out that she's there, then we can call Jason and let him know. What do you think?"

"I see your reasoning." Mary nodded. "It makes sense to me. What about Monroe? If he's going to try to see Jessica, tomorrow would be the day. It'll take quite some time to check things out at this property."

"I agree. That's why I'm thinking it might be best if we split up, one of us trails Monroe to see where he goes, and the other one checks out the property." Suzie drank more of her tea.

"Following Monroe could be touchy. Jason did warn us away from speaking to him again." Mary pursed her lips.

"I know, but we won't speak to him. It's just about seeing where he goes, and again reporting back to Jason what we find. If you don't think it's a good plan though, it's okay, you can tell me the truth." Suzie patted the back of her friend's hand. "I don't want you doing anything that you don't want to do."

"It's not that I don't want to do it, it's just that I wonder if we do find something, what will we do then? What if he meets up with Jessica and they're both about to take off? Shouldn't I stop them?"

"No." Suzie looked sternly into her eyes. "I mean that, Mary. The risk is too great. You're not to inter-fere with anything they are doing. If you see him with someone you believe is Jessica, call Jason right away. He will get someone out to you quickly, but do not do anything to keep them there, or alert them to your presence. If anything ever happened to you, I could never forgive myself."

"Just keep in mind that the same applies to you." Mary placed her hand on top of her friend's, which still rested on her own. "Are you going to be just as careful?"

"Don't worry, Mary, I will be careful." Suzie gave her hand a light squeeze.

CHAPTER 11

*E*arly the next morning, Suzie and Mary prepared travel cups of coffee and headed out for their separate tasks. Just before Mary got into the car Suzie gave her a warm hug.

"Remember what I said, keep your distance."

"I will. And you be careful, too." Mary gave Suzie a light poke on the shoulder.

"I probably won't find anything other than an empty house, but I'll keep you up to date." Suzie waited until Mary was out of the driveway before she started the car up. It was nerve-wracking to see her drive away on her own. It wasn't that Suzie didn't think she was capable of handling things herself, she knew she was, but she cared about her so much she couldn't help but be protective of her.

On the drive to Sophia's property, Suzie rolled the facts that she knew through her mind. She was certain that the murder had to be motivated by something in the book. It was obvious the book revealed the truth about something that several people didn't want aired. But what could be so bad that someone would be willing to murder over it? The time slipped by as she continued to mull over the possibilities. No matter how she spun it she couldn't quite make the pieces fit. Something was still missing. Was it Sophia?

Suzie might show up at the property only to discover that there was no one there at all. A part of her wished she was back in Garber with Mary, tailing Monroe. At least then they would be together. But her instincts told her that Sophia would be there, or at least had recently been there, and might have left a clue for her to follow to her closest location.

As Suzie navigated through the last few turns that led to the house, she discovered that the house was located at the end of a very long country road. It would be the perfect hideout for anyone attempting to dodge the law. She decided to park near the end of the driveway and walk up, as she was sure that the sound of the engine would alert anyone who was inside. When the locks clicked shut on the car, she realized she was also making herself very vulnerable. It would take some time for her to get back to the cover of the car if she faced any danger.

As Suzie approached the house, she began to lose hope that anyone was inside. It was two stories with a large attic that could have served as a third story. The windows were tall, wide, and barren of any sign of human life. The wood on the porch hadn't been treated in a long time, and one section of the railing that led up the stairs was detached. What once had likely been majestic gardens, were just piles of crumpled brown remains. It looked as if it hadn't been lived in for years. Despite the neglected appearance, all of the windows were intact. There didn't seem to be much damage to the exterior of the house. It was likely livable with a little cleaning. She could picture how beautiful it must have once been and wondered why anyone would leave it to rot away.

Cautiously, she walked around the property. When she tried a doorknob on the back door, she found it locked tight. She walked back around to the front, past wilted gardens and dried up grass. When she reached the front she decided to knock, just to give whoever might be inside some warning. She didn't want to startle them. After a few solid knocks she realized that no one was going to answer the door. If there was someone inside, they obviously didn't want company. However, that wouldn't deter her from trying to find out the truth. Her best guess was that there was no one in the house at the moment. She simply didn't sense the presence of another person. Of course, that didn't mean that no one was there, but she decided to trust her instincts. After finding the front door was locked up as tight as the back, she took another walk around the house to see if there was another way in. Every window she tried was also locked. She noticed that the locks appeared to be fairly new.

Why would anyone replace the locks if no one lives here? Maybe to keep vandals out. Suzie considered that as she neared the backyard again. A house as isolated as this could easily become a residence for squatters. Perhaps the new locks were just a precaution to prevent them from getting inside. Or maybe, it was to keep other people out, people like her, that might come snooping.

Suzie was nearly to the other side of the house

when the tip of her shoe caught on something solid beneath a pile of vines. Upon closer inspection, she realized that the vines had been gathered there, they didn't just grow naturally. She pulled the vines back and found that they moved easily. Beneath them was a pair of sloped metal doors. Clearly it was access to a basement of some kind. She also discovered that the dirt around the frame of the doors had been scuffed and overturned recently. Someone had been there, someone had moved the vines, and she guessed, someone had opened those doors. To her surprise the doors were the only entrance to the house that didn't have a lock. She gave one of the doors a tug and found it swung open easily, though a disturbing groan did escape the hinges.

Beyond the entrance were narrow, stone steps that led down into thick darkness. She flicked on the flashlight on her phone and directed it down the steps. From what she could tell there was no one in the basement, but there were tell-tale signs of a recent presence. Muddy footprints on the steps, a few bags at the base of the steps, and a lantern that hung just a few inches from the entrance. At the moment, she assumed that no one was inside as the loud door would have likely alerted anyone hidden there to her presence.

Suzie's heart pounded against her chest as she considered heading down inside. She had come here to find out the truth, hadn't she? If the truth was at the bottom of those steps, she needed to know. However, there were very few things more frightening than the dark basement of an abandoned house that might just belong to a murderer.

Suzie held her phone tightly in her hand and began down the first few steps. The glaring light illuminated a pile of paper plates, a grocery bag full of non-perishable items, and a blanket and pillow tossed across a cot. Clearly, someone had been living here. Was it Sophia? A few more steps brought her to the cement floor of the basement. Something small and quick darted past just outside of the beam of the flashlight. The movement took her breath away, and her guess that it was likely a rat didn't exactly settle her nerves. However, she continued to investigate. If she noticed anything strange, she would run right back up the steps. She was sure she could easily escape anything that jumped out at her. However, what she didn't expect was the sound of footsteps on the stairs just behind her.

Suzie spun around with the flashlight in her hand, and her heart in her throat. As the figure reached the bottom of the steps, she seemed just as startled to see Suzie.

"What are you doing in here?" The anger in her voice caused it to become high-pitched.

Suzie grew dizzy with fear as she realized she was trapped, as far as she knew there was no other way out of the basement. If there was a door that led into the house, she had no idea where it was.

"What are you doing here?" The woman's voice shook as she stared at Suzie from a few steps up.

"Sophia?" Suzie froze, her heart in her throat. The woman had plenty of advantage. She could easily attack her with any weapon she might have concealed in the purse that hung over her shoulder.

"How do you know my name?" Sophia descended the last few steps, her eyes narrowed. "Wait, I know you."

"You do?" Suzie's heart pounded. She had no idea if Sophia had gotten a good look at her the day of the murder, before she ran off down the beach.

"Yes, and I know why you're here." Sophia paused about a foot away from Suzie. "You think I did it, don't you?"

"I don't think anything. I was just curious about this place. I thought it was empty. I thought I might make an offer on it." Suzie cleared her throat. "You're the owner, aren't you?"

"Don't do that, please, don't make things up." Sophia sighed. "I'm so overwhelmed already. I can't take any more."

"Sophia, I'm not here to make things harder on you." Suzie did her best to relax her expression and her muscles. As frightened as she was, she could tell that Sophia was even more afraid. Was she terrified that she was about to be found out? "I just want to know what really happened to Amelia."

"So do I!" Sophia gulped back a sob and threw her hands into the air. "That's all I want. Don't you see? That's why I'm still here. I can't leave without knowing what happened to Amelia. But I knew, I knew you saw me that morning, and I knew that the police would be after me. So yes, I've been hiding, but not because I did anything wrong."

"I know that when you lost your mother she left the property to Amelia, and Amelia refused to sell it to you for the amount you could offer. I can only imagine how frustrating that must have been for you."

"At first, yes, I'll admit I was upset. It was so unfair of her to want to keep that property from me. It's special to me, and all she cared about was getting enough cash to help fund her book." Sophia rolled her eyes, then shook her head. "But I would never do anything to hurt her. I tried to warn her that writing about that kind of stuff would have dire consequences. She didn't want to listen to me. She said she had an obligation to reveal the ins and outs of the industry and the truth about what was going on at the company, no matter what the cost was."

"That was quite noble of her." Suzie backed up a step, but kept her voice low, and soothing.

"Noble? No, she just wanted the attention. She had a rough time of it, you know." Sophia frowned. "Poor Amelia."

"It must have been hard for you to watch her spiral the way she did. To go from a good career to typing out a conspiracy story."

"It wasn't a conspiracy. It was the truth, that much I know. She didn't tell me exactly what it was about, but I know it was true. But yes, she was obsessed with it. Even while my mother was very ill, her focus was only on that book. My mother, who practically raised her, was dying, but she couldn't be bothered to look away from that book. Yes, I was upset." Sophia's eyes widened as she looked into Suzie's. "But I didn't kill her, I would never."

"You're right. I saw you there that morning."

Suzie's heartbeat quickened as she knew that revealing that tidbit of information might put her at a higher risk of attack.

"I know, I saw you chasing after me." Sophia bit into her bottom lip, then shook her head. "I know how it must have looked to you, how it looks now. But I was only there to try to reconnect with her. She didn't want to have anything to do with me."

"Why would you want to reconnect with someone who took a restraining order out against you?" Suzie crossed her arms as she studied the woman. Her sorrow seemed genuine, but her reaction was chaotic. Was she sad because her cousin was dead, or because she had killed her?

"Amelia and I were like sisters growing up. We would spend every summer together here with my mother. It wasn't until we were adults that we grew apart. We just got busy with our lives. Then, when my mom got sick, and Amelia wouldn't help me with her, I got angry. The inheritance was just another reason to be upset with her. I lost it, I'll admit it. I was calling her all the time, and following her, just trying to get her to listen to reason."

"But she wouldn't listen." Suzie glanced past her at the stairs. She wasn't sure that she could make it past her, or that it would be wise to try, but she felt as if she needed to have an escape planned.

"No, of course she wouldn't. She was always the more stubborn one of the two of us." Sophia stepped past Suzie and farther into the basement. "Would you like something to drink? I have water." She turned towards a bag of groceries.

It was the perfect opportunity for Suzie to bolt up the stairs and back through the door, but it didn't seem to her that Sophia posed any immediate threat. Maybe if she could get some more information out of her, she could determine once and for all whether she was the killer.

"Thanks, I'll have a water." Suzie took the bottle that Sophia offered. "It must have been so hard for you to see someone you were so close to betray you like that."

"It was. But it's far harder now to think that she died believing that I was still angry with her. I'll never have the chance to make things right with her." Sophia leaned back against the wall and closed her eyes. "Look, I know you're here because you suspected me. I'm surprised you were even able to find me. And I'm sure you're chomping at the bit to tell the police about me." Sophia opened her eyes and looked into Suzie's. "But I didn't do this. I loved my cousin. I wanted to fix things between us. I was there that morning just to check on her. She wouldn't answer my calls, or my e-mails. I was worried. I guess I was right to be. I can't expect you to believe me."

"Turn yourself in to the police and tell them the truth if you're innocent." Suzie kept her voice as calm as she could. "If you didn't hurt your cousin, then you should have nothing to be afraid of, right?"

"Wrong." Sophia frowned. "I have a history with her. I was there that morning. If I were the police, I'd lock me up and throw away the key. I can't go to the police. They will never believe me, just like you don't."

"I don't know what to believe. But I know that you can't hide here forever, and the longer you do, the more guilty you look. Sophia, let's take care of all of this. Let's clear the air."

"I can't." Sophia sniffled. "I would never survive in jail. I mean, look at me." She gestured to her slim figure. "They'll eat me alive."

"If you didn't kill your cousin, then you're not going to jail." Suzie offered her hand with a reassuring smile. "I have someone you can talk to. Just come with me." Suzie knew that if she walked away from Sophia, she would find a way to disappear, and she might never face justice for the murder of her cousin. No, she couldn't be certain that Sophia killed Amelia, but she knew there was enough evidence to suspect her and she couldn't let her slip away.

"You know someone?" Sophia wiped at her eyes. "Someone who will listen to me?"

"Yes, I do. Let's go. I'll drive you myself." Suzie's heart fluttered at the offer. Was it wise to give a murder suspect a lift? If Sophia thought she trusted her, she was more likely to agree to turn herself in.

"All right, yes, it's for the best." Sophia gathered a few items.

"How long have you been here?" Suzie swept her gaze over the contents of the basement that she could see. Nothing seemed too out of the ordinary, but she knew that Jason could get a warrant to search for any evidence.

"Since the morning Amelia died. I didn't know where else to go." Sophia clutched her purse and looked at Suzie. "Go ahead up, I'll be right behind you."

"You first." Suzie took a step back and gestured to the stairs. She had no intention of turning her back to the woman.

"You think I did it, don't you?" Sophia's eyes

widened as she stared at her. "But I didn't, I didn't!" Her voice grew so high-pitched that Suzie winced.

Suzie placed her hand on the woman's back and gave her a light push towards the stairs.

"It doesn't matter what I believe, Sophia, all that matters is the truth."

CHAPTER 12

As Mary turned on the SUV, her heart fluttered. She had never been that confident about her driving, despite shuttling two kids between what seemed like thousands of activities. She preferred it when her ex-husband was able to drive instead of her. Of course, in none of those situations was she actively following a murder suspect. She did her best to keep some distance, but that only wore on her nerves more, since she was certain that at every turn and red light, she would lose sight of him completely.

Mary began to wish that Suzie was with her trailing Monroe. After a few minutes, she noticed that Monroe appeared to know exactly where he was going, and intended to get there quickly. He

139

wove between cars, and pushed past the speed limit on several occasions. After some time, he turned onto the highway. Mary braced herself for the faster speeds and thicker traffic. After she flipped on the radio in the hopes that some music would help her to relax, she settled in for a long drive. If he had to take the highway to get where he was going, she was sure it was a good distance.

Several minutes slipped by before he took an exit. She trailed his car, a few car lengths behind him. When a car turned between them, she breathed a sigh of relief. But that relief was short lived as he turned into a nearby parking lot. She had a split-second decision to make, either follow him in and risk blowing her cover, or continue past and risk losing sight of him and where he might be going. She decided to turn in right behind him. It wouldn't be that unusual for two cars to turn into a motel just off the highway, would it? He had already parked, and she had to make a move, or she would really draw attention from the cars behind her blaring their horns.

Mary followed him into the parking lot but continued past his car to the other end. As she parked, she stared in the rearview mirror at Monroe's car. She could see him climb out and head to the motel room in the middle of the strip. She held her breath, as if he might detect the shallow sound and realize that he was being watched. When he reached the door, he did give a glance over his shoulder in her direction, as if he might feel her eyes on him. But he turned back to the door and knocked. She closed her eyes for a moment. If she stayed in the car, she knew that she wouldn't see much of anything. All she would know was that he was at a motel room. She could call Jason and let him know, but by the time he arrived, whoever was inside might be gone. She decided it was important just to get a closer look. When she opened her eyes again, she saw him disappear inside. She had missed her chance to see who might have opened the door, but then from her position, she probably wouldn't have been able to tell.

As quietly as she could, Mary stepped out of the car and headed towards the motel room. Each of the rooms had thick curtains that covered the windows. None of them were open, including the one that Monroe had disappeared into. She was nervous, but she managed to walk right up to the motel room, then continue past it. She lingered a few inches away from the window and listened.

It wasn't difficult to hear what was happening

inside, as the voices were loud. One she recognized as Monroe's, the other she guessed belonged to Jessica.

"What are you doing here?" He shouted the question.

"It's none of your concern, Monroe. How did you even know I was here?"

"Someone snooping around recognized your picture. You took a tour of the bed and breakfast where Amelia was staying? Why would you do that?"

"I did what I had to do."

"I told you I would take care of it!" Monroe's voice rose even louder, and Mary jumped at the sound of a heavy thump. Had he hit her? The wall? A table? She couldn't be sure, but it sent her heart racing.

"Never mind, it doesn't matter now, does it? The story is never going to get out."

"Because she is dead! Who do you think they are coming after? Was that part of the plan too, Jessica? To get rid of me by pinning Amelia's death on me?"

"Monroe! I had nothing to do with Amelia's death. Do you really think I'm capable of something like that? Can you really look at me and tell me that you think I'm a murderer?"

"I don't know what to think! You lied about coming here, didn't you? You didn't even tell me what you were up to. You knew I was coming here to warn her about the lawsuit."

"Which I told you was a stupid idea from the beginning. I knew if you warned her, she'd just lawyer up and come after us, again. So why would you do something like that? I tried to stop you, but you wouldn't listen. I had to find out what she was really up to, how much she really planned to reveal. Why wouldn't I do that? She was known for her dramatics. She claimed to have so much information about us, but I was willing to bet she didn't have nearly as much as she pretended to have."

"So, what did you do, break into her room?"

"No, I couldn't. That woman who gave me the tour, watched me like a hawk. She wouldn't let me near Amelia's room. That's it, that's all I did. Then when I heard Amelia was dead, I got scared. I didn't know what to do. I figured I'd better just lay low for a while."

"Why didn't you tell me that you were here? Why didn't you call me?" Monroe asked.

"I didn't know what happened to Amelia." Jessica's voice trembled as she spoke. "I was afraid."

"You think I did this?"

"Didn't you?"

"No!" Monroe shouted, and something thumped again. "I'm not a murderer, Jessica!"

"Maybe not, but you're an idiot. You do realize you probably led the police right to me, don't you?"

"No, I didn't, I was careful."

"There is no way to be careful enough during a murder investigation. You have to get out of here, and fast, before the cops see us together. They're going to think that we did this together, that it was our plan from the start."

"Oh Jessica. I knew we should have left all of this alone from the beginning. We should have stopped all of this when Amelia started suspecting us."

"Keep quiet! Just keep quiet! I need to think."

Mary shifted from one foot to the other as she tried to memorize every word that was spoken. She knew that Suzie would want to hear every detail. As she leaned a little closer, she felt a hand slip over her mouth, and an arm go around her waist. The warm palm pressed lightly against her lips muffled a shout, and the arm around her waist kept her from being able to run.

"Sh." Jason's voice lingered beside her ear.

"Don't make too much noise. I don't want them to be spooked."

"Jason!" She swatted at him as he pulled her back away from the door.

"Watch it." He frowned as he batted her hands away. "What are you doing here?"

"What are you doing here?" Mary shot back.

"My job." Jason gestured to the shield on his belt. "I've been tailing Monroe, hoping that he would lead me to Jessica. Imagine my surprise when I realized I was tailing you, too." He folded his arms across his chest and stared hard into her eyes. "Your presence here could taint any evidence I collect."

"I'm sorry, Jason. I wasn't supposed to get out of the car. I just wanted to hear what they were saying."

"Mary, it's okay. But you need to be careful." His expression softened as he studied her. "Come with me." He led her away from the motel room back to her car. As they walked, she shared what she had overheard.

"I'm going to go in and speak to her. But I need to know that you're safe first. Please, go back to Dune House." Jason opened the car door for her.

"And if you see my cousin, you let her know that I need to have a conversation with her."

"Yes, okay, I will." Mary fiddled nervously with her purse. She decided against telling him where Suzie was. After all she might not have found anything at all. Once in the car, she pulled out of the parking lot under Jason's watchful eye. She was about a mile down the road when her cell phone rang. She saw that it was Suzie calling.

As Mary hung up the phone, her hand trembled. She dialed Jason's number and put the phone up to her ear. As she expected, it went to voicemail. He was probably inside the motel room speaking to Monroe and Jessica. She left a brief message requesting a call back and for him to meet them at the police station. On the drive there, her stomach churned. The thought of Suzie being alone in her car with the person who might have killed Amelia haunted her. Why had she let Suzie go there alone? She should have insisted on joining her, then at least she could have talked Suzie out of that decision. But then she might never have overheard what she did in Jessica's motel room. Maybe Suzie was safe with

Sophia, because Amelia's killer was busy with Jason.

When Mary parked at the police station, she knew it would be a bit of a wait before Suzie arrived. She headed inside and found Kirk at the front counter. He rifled through some paperwork, then glanced up at her.

"Mary, how are you?" Kirk smiled.

"A little nervous." Mary offered a smile in return, then filled him in on Suzie's plan to bring Sophia in.

"Wow, I can't believe she found her. We've been looking and hadn't been able to turn up anything. You know what, I'm going to send a patrol car to escort them in." Kirk pulled out his radio.

"Wait Kirk, what if that frightens Sophia off?" Mary frowned.

"I'll just tell them to keep a distance and no lights. If any issues come up, they'll be right there to help out." Kirk spoke into his radio, then looked back at Mary. "I hear you had a bit of an encounter yourself this morning."

"Maybe." Mary blushed as Kirk studied her.

"It's all right, I get it." Kirk closed the folder in his hand, then steered her towards his desk. "I can't let things go until a case is solved either. In fact, I just discovered that we might have another suspect we knew nothing about. I've been looking through the hate mail that Amelia received since leaving the company, and I discovered that she received several death threats. At first, I assumed they were random, sent from multiple people, then I realized that the font was the same. I've found at least five from the same sender now, and that makes me believe that someone was quite serious about doing harm to Amelia."

"Suzie said that Sophia was trying to get Amelia's attention. Are you sure they weren't from her?" Mary peered at the papers that Kirk spread out across his desk.

"I considered that, she did send some letters. Some were quite angry, but none were death threats. However, I still compared the font and the style of envelope and so forth to the anonymous death threats. The font doesn't match. It's still possible that Sophia wrote these letters using a different device, but I think it's also possible that there is someone else out there with very violent intentions." Kirk frowned as he handed some of the notes over to Mary. "Why don't you take a look? I could use another set of eyes on these, I've already had the lab go through them, but nothing was gained from that. It seems that whoever wrote these was successful at keeping them clean."

"I'll take a look." Mary looked over the paper, paying attention to every little detail. The words themselves were harsh and violent enough to make her wince, but it was those same words that surprised her. "This wasn't written by some random crazy person. This was written by someone good with words."

"I think so as well." Kirk tapped the paper with his fingertip. "The words and sentence structure seem almost professional."

"Yes, exactly." Mary rubbed her fingertip along the letters on the page. "And this wasn't printed, was it?"

"The lab says it was written on a typewriter." Kirk nodded. "They can't place the model or brand, but it definitely wasn't printed on a printer."

"Amelia used a typewriter." Mary considered that thought for a moment.

"A typewriter that's missing and was likely used as the murder weapon." Kirk sat back in his chair.

"What if—" Mary's voice trailed off as she wondered if she should really vocalize what she thought.

"Hmm?" Kirk met her eyes. "What is it, Mary?"

CINDY BELL

"Well, it's a bit strange." Mary shifted in her chair.

"I'd still like to hear it. Some of the best theories come out of the strangest places. So, let's hear it." Kirk folded his hands on the desk between them.

"What if Amelia wrote them?"

"Amelia?" His brow furrowed. "Why would she do that?"

"Maybe to generate more attention around her book." Mary shrugged, then shook her head. "Like I said, it's pretty strange, and probably not true."

"It's certainly something to consider." Kirk made a note on the pad in front of him.

"Mary." Jason paused in front of Kirk's desk, his expression stern. "I just got your message. Is Suzie here yet?"

"No, she's on her way." Mary slid back in her chair, she could tell that Jason was not pleased.

"I don't know why she wouldn't just call me to have me come and collect Sophia. Why would she take that unnecessary risk?"

"Maybe she thought it would spook Sophia." Mary chewed on her bottom lip for a moment, then looked straight at Jason. "If she did this, she had a reason to do it. I trust Suzie's judgment."

"I trust her, too, but this is just too much of a risk—"

"Jason." Kirk tipped his head towards the hall-way. "Here she is now."

Suzie and Sophia walked towards Kirk's desk, as Jason turned to face them.

"Just a second." Suzie held up her hand before he could speak. "Sophia agreed to come in and speak with you because I told her I knew people she could trust in the police department. Is that okay?" She met his gaze.

"Suzie." Jason hesitated, then frowned. "Yes, of course it's okay. Sophia." He offered his hand to the other woman. "I'd like to hear anything you have to say."

As Jason led her off to an interrogation room, Kirk followed after him.

Mary stood up from her chair and gave Suzie a light shove on the shoulder.

"What in the world were you thinking getting into a car with a murder suspect?"

"I know, I know." Suzie wrung her hands. "Trust me, it wasn't my best decision. But it got her here, didn't it?" She glanced over at her friend. "I'm a bundle of nerves to be honest."

"The important thing is that you are safe." Mary

slipped her hand into hers. "Now, let's just hope that this will lead to the truth." As they sat down at Kirk's desk together, they updated one another about the information that they'd discovered.

"So you think Jessica might be the killer?" Suzie tipped her head from side to side. "That makes sense to me, but I'm not ready to rule out Sophia just yet. She is so emotional over all of this, but I can't help wonder if that's just a front to hide her guilt, or maybe even remorse."

"Maybe. What was the car ride like with her?"

"She cried a lot. Begged me to believe that she had nothing to do with Amelia's death. Then she would get very quiet. I had the doors locked, but a couple of times I saw her grab the handle of the car door as if she might decide to jump out, but she didn't."

"That must have been so frightening."

"It wasn't easy. And weren't you supposed to stay in the car while following Monroe?" Suzie gazed at her friend with a hint of a smile on her lips. "I guess neither of us follow directions well."

"I guess not." Mary squeezed her hand. "But maybe we should try a little harder."

CHAPTER 13

When Jason emerged from the interrogation room, Suzie spotted him right away. She felt an urge to run over to him, but fought it. She knew he was probably still a little bothered about how she'd managed to get Sophia there. Instead she lingered beside Kirk's desk, and gave Mary's foot a light nudge.

Mary glanced up just as Jason began to walk over.

"Ladies." Jason folded his arms across his chest as he studied the two of them. "Why am I not surprised that you're still here?"

"I just thought you might want to share with us your thoughts about Sophia." Suzie offered him a warm smile.

153

"I have a few thoughts I'd like to share about you two being tangled up in my investigation." Jason sighed and unfurled his arms. "But there's not much point to that, now is there?"

"No." Suzie patted his shoulder. "Isn't it great to have a little extra back-up?"

"Great to have to worry about two people I care about very much getting themselves into serious trouble?" Jason shook his head. "No, there's nothing great about that."

Suzie and Mary exchanged a glance, then Suzie looked back at her cousin.

"Jason, we're both here, and we're okay. What did Sophia have to say? What do you think of her story?" Suzie took a step closer to him.

"I think she doesn't have an alibi, and she has plenty of motive." Jason scratched his fingertips back through his hair. "She claims to be heartbroken, but it could just be an act."

"She did turn herself in, though." Suzie narrowed her eyes. "That has to count for something, doesn't it?"

"Maybe." Jason pursed his lips. "Or maybe she realized that you'd discovered her, and decided her best option to make herself look good was to turn herself in."

"It's possible." Suzie nodded slowly. "She certainly hasn't been able to prove her innocence and she had plenty of time to do so."

"Right now, I'm still stuck at a dead end." Jason shook his head. "Do me a favor and keep yourself safe, all right?"

"I'll do my best." Suzie smiled. "We're just going to head back to the house, right Mary?"

"Right." Mary nodded. "No worries, Jason."

"No worries." Jason looked between both of them, then rolled his eyes. "Somehow I doubt that."

As Jason walked off Suzie linked her arm with Mary's.

"Time to figure out exactly how Sophia is involved in all of this."

"I'll meet you at the house." Mary winked at her, then headed for the door.

Suzie glanced back over her shoulder as Jason disappeared back into the interrogation room. A little research couldn't hurt anything, could it?

On the drive home, Suzie went over in her mind everything that Sophia confessed about her relationship with her cousin. So, they had a falling out. Was it possible that Sophia really was trying to mend fences with her cousin? There certainly didn't seem to be any evidence of that. In fact, if she felt the need to skulk around outside of Dune House instead of going to the door and knocking that indicated to her that she knew she would not be welcomed. However, whoever killed Amelia had been allowed into not only Dune House, but Amelia's own room. Perhaps she had decided to give Sophia a chance? Would that have been enough reason for Amelia to let her in?

Suzie pulled into the parking lot of Dune House and sat behind the wheel for a few minutes. She couldn't figure out a single reason why Amelia might have let Monroe in. Unless, he had something over her, that might compel her to open the door. She still didn't know exactly what the company was up to that caused such controversy.

When Suzie stepped into the house, she found that Mary was already there with a small lunch for them.

"I'm starving, are you hungry?"

"Yes." Suzie sighed as she slumped down in a chair. "And exhausted."

"I bet. It must have been so scary when you realized that she was right behind you. Oh Suzie, it makes me scared just thinking about it." Mary sat down across from her.

"I know, it was a stupid move on my part. I never should have been that reckless. But in the end, it didn't lead to anything dangerous. Unfortunately, it also didn't lead to any beneficial information." Suzie rubbed her hands together, then picked up the sandwich that Mary prepared for her. "Thank you for this."

"You're welcome. I don't think that it's led to nothing, though. Now we know that the cousins once had a close relationship. That might have been enough reason for Amelia to open the door for Sophia. There also might be enough motive for Sophia to have attacked her."

"Okay, but if Sophia did it, why would she take the typewriter and the manuscript with her? She had nothing to do with the company, right? So, why would she care about what Amelia had written." Suzie sat back as she took another bite of her sandwich. "I think we need to find out more about what the big scandal was with the company. I mean, the manuscript was taken, so my guess would be that was the reason for the murder. Someone wanted to keep that book from being released."

"And maybe Amelia was so protective of it that

she wouldn't even write on a computer. That tells me she didn't want the information getting out before it was released. If it did there would be no reason to publish the book."

"Yes, I agree. She hid out here, too. She knew she was in danger."

"Clearly, those death threats that Kirk showed me were quite detailed. From what was included I would think that the author likely knew quite a bit about her."

"We know the book is about the company, I think we need to learn a little bit more about this company." Suzie nodded.

"Monroe certainly isn't interested in telling the whole truth, and I'm sure that Jessica Cate didn't have much to say either." Mary frowned. "I wish I had the chance to speak to her myself."

"I wish you had stayed in the car like I told you." Suzie raised an eyebrow.

"This, from the person that ended up in the basement of an abandoned house with a possible killer?" Mary shook her head. "Nope, sorry, I'm not the one in trouble here."

"All right, all right." Suzie grinned. "Let me see what I can find out."

After over an hour of searching Suzie managed

to find some posts by an employee of Jessica Cate Public Relations. After a few searches she came across one that Jessica Cate's name was listed in. It went on about how Jessica Cate and her employees had been ripping off their clients. It didn't go into specifics, but it mentioned how the magazines were as much to blame as the publicists, and the truth had to be revealed.

"The owners and some employees of the company are involved in scamming the clients. Some employees have no idea what is going on. This company needs to be investigated before it ruins more lives. Their clients need to be protected. Every single person who works there, and is aware of what is really happening there, should be held guilty for what they have done. They have broken their clients' trust. They are criminals, hiding behind white collars, and so are we if we sit by and let this happen." Suzie read part of the post to herself. It was only posted last week. Could it have been made by Amelia?

"Maybe Amelia was a whistleblower." Suzie sat back in her chair just as Mary walked back through the door.

"A whistleblower?" Mary asked.

Suzie explained what she had found.

"Wow, those are some serious accusations. It sounds to me that whoever wrote that knows every detail about what happened at the company. If Amelia was making these accusations, had proof and was writing the book about it, that's a pretty strong motive. It would have ruined the company's reputation." Mary scooted over to peer at the page. "Amelia didn't write this. There's the author's name. I wonder if we can get a contact number?"

"It's right here." Suzie smiled as she pointed to a section of the page. "It's worth a shot, right?" She shrugged as she dialed the number. To her surprise, the phone only rang once before it was answered.

"Hello, this is Nina Brambrose, how may I help you?"

"Hi Nina, my name is Suzie, I'm calling in regard to the information on a post you made about Jessica Cate Public Relations."

"I'm sorry I'm not involved in that anymore." Her voice wavered.

"You're not? Why not?"

"I don't really want to answer any questions. You shouldn't either and stop asking them. You're putting yourself at risk. I'm sorry, I can't help you."

"Wait, Nina, what do you mean I'm putting myself at risk? Do you think you're in danger?"

"Listen, someone was murdered over this, okay? That's all I can tell you. Please don't call me again."

Suzie pulled the phone away from her ear and stared at Mary.

"She hung up. But she sounded scared, very scared."

"I think she heard about Amelia's death and is afraid that she might be next?" Mary frowned, then leaned closer to Suzie. "What if she is next?"

"I don't know." Suzie sighed. "I don't think she's going to give us any more information, though. She did say her name was Nina Brambrose. I'll see what I can find out about her." She started to conduct another search, but her phone rang before she could. "Hello, Nina?"

"No, this is Jason. Are you okay, Suzie?"

"Yes, I'm fine, Jason, I'm sorry." Suzie sat back in her chair. "How are you?"

"I've got some information I'd like to get your input on. Can you come down to the medical examiner's office?"

"Sure." Suzie looked across the table at Mary. "We can be there in fifteen minutes."

"Great. I'll see you then."

"Jason has some information. Let me just get freshened up and we can head out." Suzie stood up from the table and headed for the stairs. She'd been so nervous in that basement that she'd sweated quite a bit, and she wanted some fresh clothing for the visit to the medical examiner's office. Her mind spun as she wondered what information Jason might have for her.

Mary began to clean up the lunch dishes when her cell phone rang. She smiled when she saw it was Wes calling.

"Hi Wes."

"Hi Wes, is that it?"

"Um, hi darling?"

"I got a call from one of the local cops about the little adventure you went on today."

"Oh." Mary laughed. "Don't worry about that, it all worked out fine. I did overhear an argument between Monroe and Jessica though, that made me think she's up to something."

"So, it's true? You really followed Monroe? By yourself?"

"Yes, but that's not the point. The point is Jessica sounded as if she might have something to feel guilty about—"

"Mary, that is way too risky. Why would you do something like that?"

"Wes, calm down. I was perfectly safe."

"If you were perfectly safe then how were you able to hear what Jessica said? You had to have gotten out of the car."

"Well yes, I did." Mary frowned as she glanced over at Suzie as she came back down the stairs. "I'm fine, that's the important thing. But I was wondering if you could answer a quick question for me. I know that you are busy."

"I'm never too busy for you. But first you have to promise me that you're not going to do anything as risky as that again."

"It wasn't risky, I was never in danger." Mary's mind flashed back to the moment that she felt a hand over her mouth, before she knew that it belonged to Jason. Yes, in that moment she was terrified. She pushed the memory away and cleared her throat. "I am fine."

"And I am so grateful that you are. I admire how brave you are, you know that. Now, how can I help you?"

"If someone was writing threatening letters, but leaving them anonymous, would there be any way to trace where the letters had come from? Say, they were dropped in a public mailbox, instead of mailed from a home. How would you figure out who they came from?"

"All you have is the location of the mailbox. But that might be enough. Some post offices have cameras, and if the mailbox was not at a post office, but located on a street corner of some kind, then there may be cameras nearby. You'll have an approximate date of when it was picked up, and that should give you a place to start. I hope that helps."

"Yes, it does, so much. I didn't even consider other cameras nearby. Thanks Wes."

"Thank me by being more careful, okay?"

"I promise." Mary's heart warmed at the concern in his voice. The way he cared about her made her feel like the most valuable person in the world.

"What is your next step here?"

"We are meeting Jason, a perfectly safe meeting. He just wants some information from us."

"Good, that means I can breathe easy for a little while."

"Bye Wes." Mary smiled as she hung up the phone.

"Did he give you a hard time?" Suzie headed for the door.

"Yes, and no. I can't help but enjoy it when he worries about me. Is that wrong?" Mary picked up her purse and followed after her.

"No, I don't think so. It's nice to have someone

that cares that much." As they reached the porch, she glanced towards the water. "I know I worry about Paul like that, and I'm sure he worries about me, too. It's nice to know that someone cares."

"Yes, it is." Mary smiled to herself as she followed Suzie to the car.

CHAPTER 14

"*W*es is right you know." Suzie started the car, then glanced over at her friend.

"Hmm?" Mary looked back at her.

"We both took big risks today. We do need to be more careful. Either one of us could have ended up in a lot more trouble than we did." Suzie headed out of the parking lot.

"I'll admit, I was scared when Jason grabbed me. I know why he did it, but it still made me realize how vulnerable I really was." Mary adjusted her purse in her lap. "I'd be lying if I said I wasn't still a little spooked."

"After hearing Nina's voice on that phone call today, I am, too." Suzie chewed on her bottom lip.

"Monroe was ready to sue Amelia, she had been receiving death threats, and now someone who was attempting to expose the dodgy practices of the company is too frightened to even talk about it. I feel like we're really missing the mark with this. The post I found online mentioned that the magazines working with the company are involved. Maybe that's the key to this?"

"Maybe." Mary pointed to an empty spot near the front door of the medical examiner's office. There were several other cars in the parking lot. "It seems a little busy here today. I wonder why?"

"I'm not sure, but we're about to find out."

As they headed inside, they found the waiting room was peppered with police officers.

"What's going on?" Suzie looked at the receptionist behind the desk.

"High pressure to solve this case." The receptionist raised an eyebrow. "Plus there was another body found within city limits, and they're trying to figure out if it's related."

"Who is it?" Suzie's eyes widened.

"I'm not sure if it's been identified yet. A drowning victim." The receptionist winced.

"I'm sorry to hear that." Mary sighed and pressed her hand to her chest. "So awful."

"Yes, I'm afraid I can't tell you anything more, but Dr. Rose and Jason are waiting for you in her office." She pointed down the hall towards it. "Go ahead in."

"Another body?" Suzie whispered to Mary as they walked down the hall. "Maybe Nina does have a reason to be scared?"

"Maybe." Mary shivered, then knocked lightly on Dr. Rose's office door.

"Come in." Dr. Rose stood behind her desk. Jason stood next to her, his eyes locked on a file in front of him.

"Hi Summer, Jason." Mary stepped in, followed by Suzie, who closed the door behind them.

"Hi Mary, Suzie, thanks for coming in. This case is really heating up." Jason nodded.

"Do you think the other body that was found is related?" Suzie stepped closer.

"I can't really talk about that. That's not why I called you here." Jason didn't look up from the file.

"What did you find?" Suzie leaned against the desk and tried to catch a glimpse of the file open in front of him.

"An imprint on Amelia's hand," Jason explained.

"Imprint?" Mary settled in the chair in front of the desk.

"Yes, it's like her hand was cut by something. We think maybe it was jewelry. Maybe she grabbed this object during the struggle." Jason placed a picture on the table between them. "Sophia isn't revealing much. You knew Amelia better than anyone else in town. You saw her every day. Did you ever see her wearing something that looked like this?"

Suzie stared at the photograph. All it showed was her hand. It was clearly cut. The outline looked like a bird in flight. The wings were curved, rounded at the edges, as if the bird was rising up in the air.

"No. Mary?" Suzie pushed the picture towards her.

"We hardly ever saw her. She was always in her room." Mary shook her head. "But I don't recall her wearing any jewelry. I usually notice things like that, we have a safe where we offer to keep any jewelry or other valuables. So, if I had noticed that she wore jewelry I would have been sure to offer it."

"It wasn't found in her room or on her body, either." Jason sighed.

"If it didn't belong to Amelia then it's possible it belonged to the killer." Suzie sat down in the chair beside Mary.

"I can't see Monroe wearing something like that." Mary shook her head. "It looks feminine."

"It does." Jason tapped the picture lightly with his fingertip. "I'd say it was a woman's. If it did belong to the killer that might just point to our killer being a woman."

"Too bad there are two female suspects, and no jewelry to prove which one it is." Mary sighed. "But at least it's something."

"If either of you think of anything about what this could be, please make sure you let me know right away." Jason nodded.

"I will." Suzie stood up and smiled.

"If I think of anything, I will let you know." Mary stood up as well.

As Suzie and Mary headed back to the car Mary's phone beeped with a text.

"Oh, it looks like Wes has a few minutes free. Would you mind if I have lunch with him, Suzie?"

"No, not at all. I can drop you off if you want."

"That's okay he's only a few minutes away. He can pick me up and drop me off at home. He's been so busy I'm just glad I get a chance to see him. Do you want to join us?"

"No thanks." Suzie smiled at her as she opened the car door. "Enjoy."

"Where are you headed?" Mary could sense that she had her mind on something.

"I'm going to check on something at the library. I know Louis has many connections. I'm wondering if he can help me figure out who sent those letters."

"That's a great idea. Let me know if you find anything, okay?" Mary waved as Wes' car pulled up.

Suzie drove the short distance to the library and was relieved to see that Louis was inside. When she walked up to his desk, he was engrossed in something on the computer.

"What are you up to, Louis?"

"Suzie." He blushed and turned off the screen on the computer.

"What is it?" Suzie raised an eyebrow. "You don't have to be embarrassed around me."

"It's a local news group. Let's just say Dune House is a big topic right now."

"I imagine it is." Suzie sighed. "That's why I'm here. But if you're too busy—"

"No, I'm not. What can I do to help?" Louis gestured to a chair not far from his desk.

Suzie explained to him the possibility of catching the person who sent the death threats to Amelia.

"Well, some cameras are a matter of public record, so the public does have access to them. Let me see, you know what town it was sent from?"

"Yes, the postmark indicated it was from Bakersto." Suzie checked her notes on her phone to be sure that her information was correct. Mary had told her all the details she could remember from the envelopes and letters. She had tried to memorize as many details as possible as she knew they might be relevant.

"Great, that's a small town, not too many mailboxes, and not too many cameras." He typed a few things into the computer, then nodded. "There's only one camera on a public mailbox in the center of town. And the days the letters were sent?"

Suzie rattled off the dates.

"Okay, let's see, they do have some videos archived. I have two of those dates." Louis clicked a few things, then turned the screen so that Suzie could see it. "Now the problem of course is that there are several hours of footage. I'm sorry I don't think I can narrow it down more than that."

"That's all right, is there a way to make it go faster?"

He showed her how to adjust the speed. "If you need anything else, let me know."

"I will, thanks Louis." Suzie skimmed through the footage. A few people walked past, but none stopped at the mailbox. It was almost dark by the time she saw a female figure approach the box. However, her back was to the camera. Suzie glanced at a picture on her phone of Jessica Cate, then looked back at the screen. They had similar figures, but so did many women. Without being able to see her face it was impossible to tell for sure. She switched to the second set of footage. At about the same time of day, she saw the same woman approach the mailbox and drop in another letter. Again, she never turned to look at the camera. Did she know it was there?

Annoyed that she couldn't see more, Suzie still sent the details from the footage to Jason with an explanation of why he might be interested in it.

An instant later the vibration of her cell phone ringing caught her attention. She smiled to herself with relief that she had remembered to turn it to silent. Her eyes widened when she saw that the call was from Jason.

"That was fast." Suzie hurried outside, with a wave to Louis.

"I need you to stop investigating this case."

"I'm not investigating, you're the detective. I'm just trying to protect my business, Jason. I have guests due to come in this weekend and the entire town is talking about the murder at Dune House."

"Suzie, listen to me. I need you to drop this. I can't explain why right now, but you have to trust me, and just stop looking into this. Let me handle it. Can you do that?"

Suzie frowned as she paced back and forth along the sidewalk in front of her car. She didn't want to drop it. She had a solid lead with the images of possibly Jessica.

"I'm not doing anything dangerous, Jason."

"Yes, you are. You just don't realize it." His tone grew sterner.

"Jason, you're overtired, you need to get some rest." Suzie walked towards her car.

"I am not overtired, okay yes I am, but that is not why I am saying this."

"Okay, I hope the information I sent you will help." Suzie fought against the urge to argue with him. Sometimes she forgot that he was the detective in the family, not her. But at the same time, she knew the case was leading to more and more dead ends, and with impending guests, she couldn't risk losing her business due to the case going unsolved.

"It will. Thanks for understanding, Suzie."

Suzie stared at the phone after he hung up. Was his demand a result of the second death that might be related to Amelia's? With this still on her mind, she drove back to Dune House.

CHAPTER 15

*a*s Suzie walked in the door to Dune House, her cell phone rang again. She expected it to be Jason with more of an explanation for his demand, instead it was a number she didn't recognize. It was local, but she couldn't recall it belonging to anyone that she knew. Hesitantly, she answered.

"Suzie, it's Bill from the docks. Remember me?"

"Yes, of course I do, Bill. Is everything okay with Paul?" Suzie's heart clenched. He was supposed to be back that evening.

"Yes, as far as I know. He's still scheduled to come in tonight, maybe a little early. I called because we found something strange down here. I thought you might want to check it out." Bill

177

lowered his voice some as if he thought someone else might be listening. "I put a call into Jason, but he's caught up with something at the moment. You told me to let you know if I saw anything suspicious, so this is me letting you know."

Suzie smiled at Mary as she stepped through the door, then put the phone on speaker.

"Thanks Bill. What have you found?" Suzie already had her purse in her hands.

"Is it about Amelia?" Mary whispered, her eyes wide.

"You'll have to come see for yourself. It might be nothing. It's in the slip right next to the office. One of the fishermen brought it in today. I'm just not sure what to make of it. I have to head home to the wife, but if you want to take a look, feel free."

"Thanks Bill, I'll do just that." Suzie ended the call, then looked into Mary's eyes. "Something was found out on the water, we've got to go check it out before it gets too dark."

"All right, let's go." Mary grabbed her purse, which she had only set down moments before.

Pilot raced towards the door the moment they headed for it.

"All right, Pilot, let's go, we can go for a walk."

Suzie patted her hip. "We don't need to take the car."

"I'll grab his leash." Mary snatched it off the hook by the door. As they left, Mary was careful to lock the door behind her. It was now a habit to do so.

"Did everything go okay with Wes?" Suzie glanced at her.

"Yes, it was very nice, actually. He's closed his case and asked if he could join us and Paul for dinner tonight."

"That would be lovely. Let's try to take the same path that we think the killer did, maybe we'll notice something along the way." Suzie tipped her head towards the opening in the trees that led to the docks.

"Good idea, but we should hurry." Mary held tightly on to Pilot's leash as she followed after Suzie.

"I'm not seeing much here. I know Jason ordered the entire area to be searched, I guess they didn't leave anything behind."

As Suzie, Mary and Pilot reached the docks, the last of the daylight slipped away. Light poles dotted the long wooden expanse in sparse succession. There were plenty of shadows to hide in. Suzie had been to the docks hundreds of times, yet this time it felt very different. There were very few people around, and as the water lapped at the wooden pillars, the sound created a sense of loneliness within her.

"That must be it, Suzie." Mary led the way to the slip by the office. From a distance it appeared empty. "What is it?"

"That is a boat, or at least, some wood trying to be a boat." Suzie sunk her hands into her pockets as she stared at the craft. It was slightly wider than a canoe, but far shorter, and a single paddle rested in the middle of it.

"How can we be sure this has anything to do with Amelia's death?" Mary poked the edge of it with her foot.

"We can't, but it's certainly something we can check out. It has to belong to someone, right?"

"There's nothing in it but a paddle, though." Mary shivered as a cool wind blew off the water. "What can it tell us?"

"We know that the killer left the house and took that path towards the docks. I guess they had a boat or a car waiting for them. It's not often that a random boat is found floating out in the water. There haven't been any storms lately to set any loose. So no, it doesn't tell us much, but it's something." Suzie crept to the edge of the dock. "Maybe if we get inside we'll find something. It could be just a crumpled piece of paper, or a piece of fabric stuck to the wood."

"Okay, let's take a look." Mary grabbed the railing on the dock while Suzie stepped through the small opening.

The wooden boat was so small Suzie wasn't sure it would seat both of them, let alone Pilot as well. It rocked gently in the mild current of the water. With every dip, she expected it might sink, but it didn't.

"I'm not sure that I would even call this a boat. I'm not sure it will hold us." Suzie pushed at the edge with her foot, not enough to tip it, but to test how solid it was.

"Somehow it ended up far from the docks. My guess is that someone had it tied somewhere, or maybe even attempted to anchor it, and somehow it broke loose." Mary reached down and grabbed a frayed rope that was tied near the front of the boat. "See?"

"Yes, I think you're right. I bet that the killer tried to hide it somewhere, but it got loose." Suzie ran her fingertips along the rim of the boat and raised an eyebrow as she drew her hand back. "Look at this."

"Is that ink?" Mary studied the smudges on her skin.

"I believe it is." Suzie's gaze returned to the boat. It didn't matter if it wasn't sturdy, she was determined to get on board. As she climbed in, Mary did her best to hold the boat steady for her.

"Anything?" Mary watched as Suzie inspected the inside of the boat. "Reeds." She pulled them out from underneath her feet. Then she glanced around the open harbor. Off to the far side of the harbor was an outcropping from the woods that was laden with reeds. "That way."

"Hold on, let me come with you. Let me just take Pilot back." As Mary said the words, Pilot launched into the boat.

The entire boat rocked back and forth, in such a way that made Suzie cry out and grasp the edges. Pilot sat down, his tail wrapped around him, and gazed up into Suzie's eyes.

"Sure Pilot, that didn't rock the boat at all."

"I guess we all might as well go." Mary heaved herself into the boat before Suzie could stop her.

"Easy! Careful!" The boat rocked wildly for a moment, then settled. Pilot wagged his tail happily between them.

"What if this thing sinks? Should we get life-jackets?" Mary gripped the edges of the boat.

"That section of the harbor is similar to a swamp. Paul never takes his boat down there because he says it's too shallow. Even if it does sink, we should be all right." Suzie grabbed the sole paddle in the boat and began to steer the boat away from the dock. She continued to paddle. It didn't take long for them to disappear into the tall reeds. The water was so shallow that there were places that Suzie had to use the paddle to push against the sandy bottom.

"There." Mary pointed to a small structure that looked similar to a shack. Tied to the lop-sided old dock in front of it, was the remainder of the rope.

"That must be where the boat was stored!" Suzie began to push the paddle through the water quickly.

"Suzie!" Mary gasped as she pulled her feet back towards her. "My shoes are soaked."

"I'm sorry I didn't mean to splash you." Suzie continued to paddle.

"No, you didn't splash me, Suzie. There's a hole in the boat!" Mary pointed to the large puddle that had gathered between their two seats. "We're going to sink!"

"It's okay, don't worry. We're not very deep, we can wade to that little patch of land."

"And then what?" Mary met her eyes. "We already have no signal out here."

"It's okay, we'll figure it out once we're on land."

Pilot sniffed at the water, gave a sharp yelp, then jumped out onto a small strip of land. It was too narrow for all of them to fit.

"Pilot, don't!" Suzie stood up as the dog took off along the strip of land. "Pilot, come back!"

"Suzie! The boat!" Mary grasped the sides as the boat began to sink. "We have to get out of here or we might get tangled up in it. We can go on the land from the other side and get to Pilot from there."

"You're right." Suzie reluctantly looked away as Pilot disappeared into the tall reeds. She turned her attention back to the boat. The water was above her ankles already. "You first, Mary. We're just going to have to wade through the water. I'm sorry."

"It's okay, I can do it, Suzie, don't worry." Mary began to ease herself up into a crouched position. Before she made it all the way up, a figure appeared at the edge of the patch of land, covered in a long cloak.

"Who is that?" Suzie ignored the fact that the water crept up along her calves as she stared.

"Catch this!" The figure tossed some rope in their direction. The voice was distinctly feminine, but Suzie didn't recognize it. After a moment's hesitation, she grabbed the rope.

"Suzie." Mary looked up at her, her eyes wide. "You know—"

"I know." Suzie frowned. "But we have nowhere else to go." She bent over and tied the rope to the boat. A moment later the figure began to pull the boat towards the land. With every foot that passed Suzie's heart sank with dread. The closer she came to the person on the edge, the more certain she became that she recognized her.

CHAPTER 16

"Where are they?" Paul paused at the edge of the porch and stared down at Wes.

"I don't know." Wes pulled his hat off and ran his hand back over his head. "I've called Mary several times, and she hasn't answered. I tried Suzie as well and her phone went straight to voicemail."

"We should tell Jason." Paul descended the steps to the parking lot, and glanced back once over his shoulder. "I don't think Pilot is in there, either."

"I already called Jason. He said he hasn't heard from either of them, and as far as he knew their only plans were to relax and have a quiet afternoon." Wes narrowed his eyes. "Which makes me even more worried."

"You're right, those two and a quiet afternoon don't exactly go together." Paul shoved his hands into his pockets. "We need to figure out where they went. Mary didn't send you any texts or anything that might give you a clue?"

"No, I haven't heard from her since I dropped her off here after lunch." Wes shifted from one foot to the other. "I did come down on her rather hard when I heard about her following Monroe. I shouldn't have done that."

"Hey, you were just looking out for her." Paul placed his hand on his shoulder. "You can't blame yourself for that."

"Maybe if I hadn't been so firm about it, she would have been willing to tell me where she and Suzie were going." Wes closed his eyes briefly. "Sometimes I forget just how capable those two are."

"Yes, me too. But Suzie will never let me forget it for long. Look, we know they were investigating Amelia's murder. Which means they likely followed a clue somewhere. But where?"

"Sophia was recently released from custody. Jason didn't have enough to hold her. It's possible that they went back to her house to speak to her or look for more evidence. Maybe we should check there first, but that's a long distance." Wes shook his head. "If we go there, and we're wrong, and they're in trouble, what then?"

"I think we should stay local. I doubt that Suzie and Mary would have gone too far with Pilot in tow. Plus, their cars are here. Wherever they went, they must have walked." Paul scratched his cheek. "What about Monroe and Jessica?"

"Wait a minute, Mary said they were leaning more towards the possibility that Jessica was the one who sent the death threats to Amelia. She said that Suzie was at the library trying to figure out who had sent the letters. Maybe Louis knows something?" Wes snapped his fingers.

"I'll bet he does."

"I'll call him right now." Wes dialed his number, and tried not to notice the way his finger shook as he did.

"It's just not like Suzie not to text or call, she knew I was coming home. I did get in a little early, but still, she usually checks in to see where I'm at. I wonder if she spoke to Bill?"

"Nothing." Wes shook his head as he hung up the phone. "Louis said that Suzie did find some information, but forwarded it to Jason right away, and then left."

"Give me just a second." Paul dialed Bill's number. After a few moments he answered. "Bill, it's Paul."

"Hey Paul, did you get in okay?"

"Sure, thanks. A little early actually. Listen, have you seen Suzie today by any chance?"

"Sure, I talked to her before I left for the night. I called her and I told her about a boat that drifted into the harbor. I thought it might have something to do with that girl's death. She told me to tell her if I spotted anything strange?"

"She did?" Paul narrowed his eyes. "Did Suzie look at it?"

"I'm not sure, she said she was going to. I had to head home. It's in the slip by the office if you want to have a look."

"Thanks, I appreciate the information."

"Is everything okay, Paul?"

"I hope so." Paul hung up the phone, then tipped his head towards the trail that led down to the docks. "They went that way, let's go." Paul took off at a jog down the path. His heart pounded against his chest almost in time with Wes' footfalls behind him. Something was wrong, he was sure of it. He didn't want to believe it, but his instincts told him that Suzie and Mary were in serious trouble.

"Hurry, maybe they're still at the docks and just not answering for some reason." Paul emerged from the path and crossed the road to the dock. His heart sank as he saw the slip by the office empty.

"Where are they?" Wes slowed to a stop beside him.

"Out there. I can see some lights." Paul gazed out across the open water, towards a patch of reeds. "We're going to need a boat."

"Don't you uh, have a boat?" Wes looked towards Paul's boat a few slips away.

"It'll never make it. We need something small, and we need it fast. Whatever those two are getting into, it's getting dark, and it's going to be hard to find them."

"I'll call Jason. The police should have their own crafts." As Wes dialed the number he looked out over the open water. "Where are you, Mary?"

As the boat made its final approach to land, Suzie tried to send a quick message to Paul to let him know where they were. However, her phone had no signal.

"Mary, can you get a call out?" She looked over at her friend as panic built within her.

"No, no service." Mary noticed a small boat tied to the other side of the dock. It was almost completely hidden in the reeds.

Mary's attention returned to the woman. She gulped back a gasp as she recognized the woman in front of them.

"Lavinia?" Suzie's eyes widened. Of all the people she expected to see it wasn't the guest from Dune House. Suzie stepped out of the boat but offered a hand back to help Mary out of it. The boat would not provide them any means for escape now that it had a hole in it. But their rescuer was no hero, she knew that for certain. Only one person would know where the boat had been hidden, only one person would have any business out in the area they had drifted to.

"Yes, it's me." Lavinia sighed as she studied her. "I guess you're wondering why I'm here?"

"Out for a stroll, I'd assume." Mary smiled. "It's a nice evening for it. We should be on our way."

"And where are you going to go?" Lavinia laughed as she looked over the murky water. "Are you going to make a swim for it? The temperature is dropping, this water is full of snakes."

"That must be your boat." Suzie offered cheerfully as she gestured to the almost completely hidden boat. "Can you give us a ride?"

"No, I'm sorry, but you're not leaving here." Lavinia tipped her head towards the small shack. "Get inside."

"No thanks." Suzie grabbed Mary's hand and pulled her back a few steps. "I'd rather stay out here."

"That's not an option. Inside, both of you." Lavinia pointed to the shed. "I have ways of making you, but it will be rather unpleasant. Don't bother trying to call anyone, there's no service out here. Don't bother trying to scream, because no one can hear you. I need all of this to be settled tonight. I need to go back to work. I need to write. I need to publish my articles. I need to get my life back."

She needed to write? Publish her articles? All of a sudden, Suzie knew exactly who Lavinia was. JuJu Lurue, the entertainment reporter.

"Lavinia, we can talk about this." Suzie took a step towards her.

"No, we can't!" Lavinia slammed her hand into Mary's back and forced her several steps forward.

"Don't touch her!" Suzie gasped as Mary cried out in pain from the sudden movement. Her knees were often sore, and she was sure this only made the situation worse.

"Then get inside, or I'll touch her again." Lavinia waved her hands and laughed.

"Okay, fine." Suzie moved past Mary to the shack. As she stepped inside, she knew it was a bad idea, but she didn't know what else to do.

"I had no intention of bringing the two of you into this, but you're here now, and there's nothing else I can do." Lavinia frowned as she followed them both inside.

"Lavinia, you're JuJu Lurue, aren't you?" Suzie stared at her as Mary gasped.

"Well done." Lavinia nodded. "I borrowed my sister's identification, her life really, so I could come here without raising suspicion."

"You didn't have to do this. Why did you kill Amelia?" Suzie stared at her as she took a step closer to them. It didn't appear she was armed, but that didn't mean she wasn't.

"I had to keep my secret."

"What secret?" Suzie asked. "Exactly, what was Amelia's book about?"

"Oh, I guess I can tell you two. It's not like you'll be able to tell anyone." JuJu smirked. "Some of the publicists would contact me with false stories about their clients. Jessica Cate was the worst. They would pay me off to write the stories, hint at what they wanted kept secret without revealing the whole story. Then the publicists would get more money from their clients to fix the problem, repair their reputation. Everybody made some extra cash. It's not like the celebrities and companies didn't have it, they were loaded. We all took advantage of the opportunity to fill our pockets, it wasn't that big of a deal."

"So, what was the problem then?" Suzie shrugged.

"Amelia somehow found out about it and she decided that she wanted in on it, but Jessica refused. Jessica denied the rumors. Amelia knew she was lying and thought she just didn't want to include her. She was furious about it and decided to turn it into something more. She wasn't trying to protect anyone, she just saw an opportunity to make some cash. First, she tried threatening Jessica, but she didn't go for it. She fired her for it. Then she decided she would write this book. No matter what anyone said, she was determined to do it. All she had to do was drop the idea of writing the book, and then everything would have been fine. But instead she continued."

"Why didn't Amelia say something when she saw you at Dune House?" Suzie asked.

"She had no idea who I was. I work remotely and she never met me. None of the publicists did. We just spoke on the phone. They sent money to my account. But Amelia couldn't leave it alone. She was going to ruin my reputation. She was going to reveal what I was doing. I would have become a social outcast. No one would contact me with their stories. My career would be over. So, I knew I had to do something to try and scare her away."

"You threatened her?" Mary asked.

"Yes, I sent her some letters that should have made her give up the idea of revealing the story. Instead she kept going. I sent more letters."

"You wrote them on a typewriter to protect yourself." Mary nodded. "So no one would be able to trace them."

"So I thought." JuJu narrowed her eyes. "However, that wasn't the case. Because the cops started sniffing around me. The ink ribbon in the typewriter would have had the imprint of the letters I had sent. It would have led straight back to me. I went to destroy the typewriter and ink before it could get me arrested for the threats and discovered that Amelia had it."

"You had to do something." Suzie nodded.

"I knew that if she figured out I was the one to write the letters she would have worked out who I was, it would have destroyed my life. I couldn't let that happen. All I wanted to do was get the ink back. I was going to get the ink and check out the next day as planned. I had it all set up."

"But Amelia never left her room?" Mary asked.

"No." JuJu shook her head vehemently. "I went to talk to her a few times, but she would never let me in. She would never leave me alone with the typewriter."

"How did you get in then?" Suzie wanted to delay her, she was still hoping that help would arrive.

"When I tried to talk to her one morning, she took ages to open the door, and she mentioned that she slept with headphones on." JuJu sighed. "So, I thought I would sneak in when she was asleep. The last time I tried to speak to her I wedged some gum into the door jam, when she wasn't looking to stop the lock from closing completely. I thought I would sneak in while she was sleeping and get the ink. But she woke up and caught me. She tried to stop me from taking it. We got into a struggle. I had no choice. I had to take care of the problem. But when

I killed her, I knew I couldn't just disappear. It would look very suspicious. I needed to play it cool for a while, wait for everything to die down. I came out here a few times with Michael, he knew about this spot and the shack from the fishermen on the docks. So, after I killed Amelia, I came out here to clean up and dump the stuff. Then I went back to Dune House before everyone woke up. I never planned to kill her, I just wanted to get the ink."

"I understand. You had to protect yourself." Mary crossed her arms as she took a step away from JuJu's approach. "But you don't need to protect yourself from us. We'll just be on our way."

"Sure, so you can run back to the police and tell them what you saw here? What I told you? No, I can't allow that to happen. I've worked too hard for all of this."

"What about Michael?" Suzie kept her gaze fixated on her, observing her every move.

"What would he think of all of this? Does he know what you did to Amelia? Or did he even help you do it?"

"Keep quiet, you don't know anything about Michael. He shouldn't have come out here." JuJu reached up to her chest, as if to grasp something, but there was nothing there. "He had nothing to do with this. He didn't even know who I was. What I had done."

Suzie noticed a smudge of faded ink that stained the skin on her arm.

"Were you going to try and make him take the fall for Amelia's murder? Are you going to pin our deaths on him, too?" Mary's voice wavered as she spoke. Fear bubbled up within her. There was no way that JuJu was going to let them live.

"Keep quiet about Michael!" JuJu roared her words so roughly that Mary jumped a step back. "I will not go to prison over this! I'm sorry, but this is over!"

As JuJu turned and stepped through the door, Mary held her breath. Was she really going to leave them there? She doubted it, but JuJu disappeared a moment later.

The door swung shut behind her, and the entire shack quaked with the force of it. Suzie heard something slide into place.

"No!" She lunged towards the door and banged against it. Though the door shook, it did not budge more than an inch. "Let us out of here!" She slammed her fists against the door. In the distance, she thought she could hear some laughter as a paddle sloshed through the water.

"We're locked in." Suzie turned back to face Mary.

"That's not the worst part." Mary stepped closer to the door. "I smell smoke."

"Are you sure?" Suzie's heart began to pound. "Maybe there's a campfire in the distance."

"No, I don't think so. It smells too strong for that. I think she might have set a fire."

"Help!" Suzie cried out as she moved towards the back wall. The fire would not take long to spread. "Someone help us!" She slammed her foot against the wood, but despite its age it was stronger than she expected. "Mary, is the phone working?"

"No, it's not, not at all." Mary gasped, then began to cough as the smoke filled the shack.

"Get low." Suzie pulled Mary down beside her, then lifted her blouse to cover her mouth. Mary did the same. "Don't worry we're going to find a way out of here." She swept her gaze through the shack. It was mostly empty, but she spotted something on the floor near the opposite wall. It looked like a long, metal pole. What it might have been used for she didn't know, but she hoped it would be enough to break through the wood. As she scrambled to get it, the heat from the fire singed her skin.

Even the pole was hot by the time Suzie grabbed

it. Luckily it was not too hot to grasp. She pulled it back to Mary's side then heaved it against the wall. The end of the pole made a small dent, but it didn't break free any of the wood. As Suzie tried to take another swing, she took a breath of the smoke-filled air and began to cough. When she dropped the pole, Mary picked it up and swung it hard against the wall. To her shock a large gap formed. Then another. She realized it wasn't the pole that had broken the wall. Instead someone on the other side had an ax.

CHAPTER 17

"Jason!" Suzie gasped as he tore down another portion of the wall.

"Give me your hand!" Jason thrust his hand through the damaged wall.

"You first, Mary." Suzie guided her friend towards the opening.

Mary grabbed Jason's hand, but reached back and grabbed Suzie's hand as well. She pulled her friend through right behind her. Once outside, Jason steered them both away from the still burning shack.

"Thank goodness you found us." Suzie wiped at tears caused by a mixture of fear, smoke, and relief.

"I couldn't have said it better." Wes rushed up to

them and threw his arms around Mary. "I was so worried about you."

"Jason, do you have them?" Paul's voice boomed from the edge of the water. "Suzie?"

"I'm okay, Paul!" Suzie ran towards him and waved at the same time, nearly tripping over her own feet to get to him.

"Suzie!" Paul stretched his arms out to her and helped her onto the small boat. "Are you hurt?" He ran his hands along her arms, then looked into her eyes.

"I'm fine." Suzie drew a deep breath, despite the fact that the air was still laced with smoke. "It was Lavinia! She's really JuJu Lurue!"

"We know." Jason stopped beside the boat, then offered his hand to help Mary onto it. "Don't worry about any of that right now, we just need to get you home and safe."

"What about the fire?" Mary looked back at the shack which was almost completely destroyed. Her heart lurched as she realized that she and Suzie had been inside of that inferno only moments before. As the boat pulled out into the water, she clung to Wes' hand.

"It should burn itself out, but a fireboat is on its way to handle the flames." Jason stood near the end of the boat and looked back at the shack as well.

When Suzie noticed him shiver, she rubbed his shoulder.

"Jason, you saved us."

"Actually, it was these two that did the saving." Jason gestured to Paul and Wes. "If it wasn't for them, I wouldn't have even known that you two were missing. What were you doing out here?" He crossed his arms as he turned to look at them.

"We just followed the path we thought the killer might have taken, but we had no idea that we might run into her. Honestly." Suzie leaned into Paul's chest as he steered the boat out into the open water.

"I believe you." Jason glanced at her, then back at the fire that could still be seen in the distance. "I'm just glad that we got to you in time. We have been looking into JuJu. We got a break on who she was just a couple of hours ago."

"You knew that JuJu did this?" Mary's eyes widened. "You knew that Lavinia was JuJu?"

"Yes, and no. With not much to go on, Kirk and I decided to start tracing the typewriter, we didn't know the make or model, but we did know that someone had given it to Amelia. Sophia told us that Amelia didn't own a typewriter, and that she had mentioned borrowing one from a friend, but she didn't know who the friend was. We figured if we could trace the typewriter to the friend, we might find out more about Amelia. Once we did, we discovered a connection between the friend, Nina Brambrose, and Judy Lurue."

"JuJu." Suzie nodded.

"Yes, she goes by the name JuJu for her job. After more investigation we found out her sister was Lavinia Robertson. The guest that was supposedly staying at Dune House during the murder. When we spoke to Lavinia, she said she knew nothing about Dune House and claimed that her identification had been stolen. Apparently, Amelia and Nina worked together at Jessica Cate Public Relations briefly. They remained friends. Nina got her cousin, Judy a job at a magazine she had contacts at, and Amelia and Nina continued their friendship. Nina loaned the typewriter to Amelia, but what Nina didn't realize was that before she lent it to Amelia her cousin had been using it on a regular basis. She never thought her cousin would be one of the reporters involved in the scandal that Amelia was going to write about."

"That must have come as a shock." Mary sighed.

"I'm sure it did." Jason nodded. "Nina was

going to help Amelia get more information about the scandal, but then she found out who was involved, and then Amelia was murdered so she backed out. We were able to positively identify the death threats that Amelia received as being typed on the same typewriter."

"JuJu said that this wasn't only about stealing the manuscript, she was also after the typewriter. The imprints left on the ribbon could have landed her in prison for the death threats. When she tried to get it back, Amelia caught her, there was a struggle, and JuJu killed her. I guess you will find out far more when you question her." Suzie straightened her shoulders as she scanned the dock. There were several police cars, two ambulances, and one loudly barking Pilot. "You found him!" She smiled as Paul navigated the boat into an empty slip.

"Him, yes. JuJu, no." Jason sighed as he turned to look at her. "She slipped away from me. I'm sorry. I can't be certain that you're safe. But we are tracking her as we speak."

"It's okay, Jason." Mary studied him for a moment. "I think I know of a way you still might be able to catch her."

"You do?" Jason helped her, then Suzie, off the boat. As the group gathered on the dock, Pilot ran up to them. He bounced back and forth between Suzie and Mary, licking their hands and whimpering with happiness.

"Lavinia and Michael were dating. Remember the shape that was cut into Amelia's hand?"

"Yes, it looked like a bird. What about it?" Jason frowned.

"I don't think it was a bird. I think it was the letter 'm'. I think it stood for Michael. Michael had a chunky, long necklace. I offered to put it in the safe for him, but he refused. I couldn't see the pendant because it was tucked under his shirt, but maybe it was the letter 'm'. He said he had something to give Lavinia, maybe he gave the necklace to her. I am sure I saw Lavinia wearing it. I didn't see it close up though. I was going to offer to put it in the safe for her, but the next time I saw her she didn't have it." Mary narrowed her eyes. "If they were close then it might be enough to draw JuJu out of hiding. Do you still have access to Michael?" She met his eyes.

"Mary." Jason cleared his throat, then forced himself to look back at her. "Michael was the drowning victim."

"What?" Mary's cheeks flushed. "Why didn't you tell us?"

"I couldn't. It needed to remain confidential

while we were hunting the murderer. That was why I wanted you to stay out of this, I knew how dangerous the murderer might be. We now believe JuJu killed Michael when he suspected or worked out that she killed Amelia. We believe he came out to the shack and she drowned him to keep him quiet. It was his boat she just used to get away."

"Oh Jason." Suzie sighed, then rubbed her cheeks. "How are we ever going to find her now?"

"It won't be hard. I have the help of someone that she won't expect. Her cousin, Nina. She has already alerted me that JuJu had called to ask if she can spend the night at her place. I was headed there when I heard the report of you two missing. I sent Kirk and a few others to pick her up." Jason glanced at his phone, then nodded. "They caught her on the way there. She's in custody. You and Mary are safe now." He smiled as he looked between them.

"What a relief." Mary grabbed Suzie's hand and squeezed it. "It's over, Suzie."

"Yes, it is." Suzie felt as if every muscle in her body relaxed, and suddenly she was ready for a nap. "Let's go home, Mary."

"Absolutely." Mary wrapped her arm around Suzie's. As Pilot walked beside them, they headed for the magnificent house on the hill above them. Finally, the truth about Amelia's death was revealed, and though it would take some time for the memory of it to fade, the important thing was that her murder was solved.

The End

ALSO BY CINDY BELL

DUNE HOUSE COZY MYSTERIES

Seaside Secrets

Boats and Bad Guys

Treasured History

Hidden Hideaways

Dodgy Dealings

Suspects and Surprises

Ruffled Feathers

A Fishy Discovery

Danger in the Depths

Celebrities and Chaos

Pups, Pilots and Peril

Tides, Trails and Trouble

Racing and Robberies

Athletes and Alibis

CHOCOLATE CENTERED COZY MYSTERIES

The Sweet Smell of Murder

A Deadly Delicious Delivery

A Bitter Sweet Murder

A Treacherous Tasty Trail

Pastry and Peril

Trouble and Treats

Fudge Films and Felonies

Custom-Made Murder

Skydiving, Soufflés and Sabotage

Christmas Chocolates and Crimes

Hot Chocolate and Homicide

Chocolate Caramels and Conmen

Picnics, Pies and Lies

Devils Food Cake and Drama

DONUT TRUCK COZY MYSTERIES

Deadly Deals and Donuts

Fatal Festive Donuts

Bunny Donuts and a Body

Strawberry Donuts and Scandal

SAGE GARDENS COZY MYSTERIES

Birthdays Can Be Deadly

Money Can Be Deadly

Trust Can Be Deadly

Ties Can Be Deadly

Rocks Can Be Deadly

Jewelry Can Be Deadly

Numbers Can Be Deadly

Memories Can Be Deadly

Paintings Can Be Deadly

Snow Can Be Deadly

Tea Can Be Deadly

Greed Can Be Deadly

Clutter Can Be Deadly

WAGGING TAIL COZY MYSTERIES

Murder at Pawprint Creek

Murder at Pooch Park

Murder at the Pet Boutique

A Merry Murder at St. Bernard Cabins

BEKKI THE BEAUTICIAN COZY MYSTERIES

Hairspray and Homicide

A Dyed Blonde and a Dead Body

Mascara and Murder

Pageant and Poison

Conditioner and a Corpse

Mistletoe, Makeup and Murder

Hairpin, Hair Dryer and Homicide

Blush, a Bride and a Body

Shampoo and a Stiff

Cosmetics, a Cruise and a Killer

Lipstick, a Long Iron and Lifeless

Camping, Concealer and Criminals

Treated and Dyed

A Wrinkle-Free Murder

A MACARON PATISSERIE COZY MYSTERY SERIES

Sifting for Suspects

Recipes and Revenge

Mansions, Macarons and Murder

NUTS ABOUT NUTS COZY MYSTERIES

A Tough Case to Crack

A Seed of Doubt

Roasted Penuts and Peril

HEAVENLY HIGHLAND INN COZY MYSTERIES

Murdering the Roses

Dead in the Daisies

Killing the Carnations

Drowning the Daffodils

Suffocating the Sunflowers

Books, Bullets and Blooms

A Deadly Serious Gardening Contest

A Bridal Bouquet and a Body

Digging for Dirt

WENDY THE WEDDING PLANNER COZY MYSTERIES

Matrimony, Money and Murder

Chefs, Ceremonies and Crimes

Knives and Nuptials

Mice, Marriage and Murder

ABOUT THE AUTHOR

Cindy Bell is a USA Today and Wall Street Journal Bestselling Author. She is the author of the cozy mystery series Wagging Tail, Donut Truck, Dune House, Sage Gardens, Chocolate Centered, Macaron Patisserie, Nuts about Nuts, Bekki the Beautician, Heavenly Highland Inn and Wendy the Wedding Planner.

Cindy has always loved reading, but it is only recently that she has discovered her passion for writing romantic cozy mysteries. She loves walking along the beach thinking of the next adventure her characters can embark on.

You can sign up for her newsletter so you are notified of her latest releases at http://www.cindybellbooks.com.

Made in the USA
Las Vegas, NV
20 May 2023

72318409R00125